Her Doctor Prince

Fiona McArthur

CHAPTER ONE -
Zafar

The elevator door opened, people spilled out into the wide foyer of Coogee's Beach Hotel and Prince Zafar Aasim Al Zamid stepped inside to hit a wall of anxiety he hadn't expected. To his disgust his heart began to pound and sweat broke out.

Several people slipped past him into the elevator. Zafar heaved a ragged breath. The doors shut.

Unexpectedly, a drift of orange soap vividly recalled the memory of fruit laden trees in the palace grounds as a child, and by association, the warmth of the memory somehow soothed him.

Scents and recollections that calmed were an excellent idea. Life had been much less complicated then. He straightened his spine and opened his eyes as the lift shifted under his feet.

Lately he'd been acquiring phobias like new bespoke shirts. Since the hijacking it had been heights, now elevators - worse every ascent - until even a closing door caused symptoms. This latest aversion seemed exacerbated by the metallic tang of brass rails and crowded lifts had become the most intolerable.

Perhaps it was a sign the claustrophobia in his life had worsened since he'd been forced to give up his work in favour of royal duty.

He would address his inner calm with the solitude of a retreat as soon as he sorted this latest mess. The vastness of the desert always made even his multitude of stressors seem less significant.

For the moment he was cramped and palpitating in a rising square box with the painful reminder of all he'd lost. With his eyes open he could see this particular enclosed space held a fragile-appearing new mother with a baby in one arm, a beaming new father clutching a balloon, and thankfully the orange-scented woman as well, dispensing an aura of tranquillity over all of them.

The metallic 'It's A Boy' helium balloon bobbed towards him and Zafar leant closer to the wall and regretted his decision to stay at this hotel. A Baby Hotel. The first and last place he needed to be. The image he carried of his tiny son's body flickered in his mind and he forced it away. Such happy families were constant reminders he could have done without, but the stakes were high.

He had hoped to find Fadia, his estranged cousin, still pregnant but time fought against him. He'd discovered she planned to convalesce here instead of the hospital should he arrive too late to find her before the new heir was born.

The lift jerked and bounced more than it should and his pulse pounded in his ears with the vertigo.

The balloon wielder tugged on the string as he hailed the woman. 'Carmen! We didn't get a chance to thank you.' He grabbed the woman's hand and shook it vigorously. 'You were amazing.'

The woman retrieved her hand and smiled at the young mother. 'Hello again, Lisa, Jock. Lisa was the amazing one.'

Her voice soothed like a cool hand to his forehead and, infinitesimally, the rise in his agitation lessened as the phobia receded. Thankfully. It would be useful if his psyche finally accepted the obscenity of irrational fears. Especially for princes of Zandorro.

'It was a beautiful birth.' She cast Zafar a swift apologetic look for their exclusive conversation, and the unexpected impact of her one compassionate glance collided as if that ridiculous balloon had bumped him, before she turned back to the father.

Medical background, he concluded, and dismissed the stab of frustration the loss of his career left him with. Midwife. He'd met women like her before – those natural soothers who could create rapport with strangers without effort.

He lifted his head and studied her. Anything was good to take his mind off the ascent through the lift well.

Thankfully his phobia retreated by the second as he perused her features. She had thick black hair coiled on her head like silken rope. A hint of Irish accent. Carmen seemed more Spanish than Irish yet she suited her name.

He watched her mouth as she smiled and spoke. 'How is young Brody?'

Jock laughed, loudly, and Zafar winced as the noise jarred his ears. 'He's a bruiser.' The father's pride resonated within the four walls like a banshee as the lift stopped at the fifth floor with an extra jolt. The cage floor fell six inches and bounced before it came back to the level. Everyone laughed nervously, except Zafar. He closed his eyes and swallowed the nausea.

Rustling and movement as the lift emptied and the father's voice, a little further away now, 'We'll see you, then.'

'I'll be down as soon as I have handover report from the morning midwife.' Ms Carmen had remained in the lift. He opened his eyes as she waved at the couple.

'That's great. We'll see you then.' Zafar noted the relief in the father's voice and his mind clutched at the distraction of wondering about this move of postnatal women from the hospital into hotels to recover from birth.

Not something he was familiar with but it made sense when he thought about benefits. A place of quiet comfort, fewer germs, useful for the hospital to have quick turnover and quite appropriate for those who could afford it.

The lift doors closed silently, though the cage remained stationary, and he stared at the lights on the panel above the door despite the insidious desire to study more closely the woman called Carmen.

She stepped back and seemed to lean into the wall.

He knew she was tall because her head came above his shoulders and her knot of hair had been near his nose as she drifted orange blossom his way. The lift still didn't move. Seconds to go and he would be able to breathe properly.

He glanced at her from under his lashes and saw her eyes were closed. He frowned. Not a usual occurrence when he shared space with a woman. In repose she appeared wilted and weary. Worn out?

His concern increased. 'Are you unwell?'

Her eyes jerked open and she straightened. 'Good grief.' She blinked at him and then focussed. 'A micro sleep. Sorry. I've been on night shift. It's been a busy week.'

Suddenly he felt empathetic to a perfect stranger because yes, he could remember that weariness from a string of busy days and nights during his internship. Lack of sleep that he'd grumbled about, but now the choice was no longer his, he'd gladly suffer from that inconvenience again.

This was the problem returning to Sydney. It brought back the dissatisfaction with the direction his life had moved. Frustration he shouldn't feel towards his duty to Zandorro.

The elevator jerked, ground upwards for a few inches, the sooner the better he thought, then the lift jolted as the cable stopped.

Come on. His breath caught as he waited. The doors didn't open and when he turned to the floor level indicator they sat on neither five nor six. Midway between floors. Stopped. Stuck.

This was not good.

His heart rate shift gear, galloped faster again before his next breath, his chest tightened, and air jammed stagnantly in his lungs.

'I am so not in the mood for this.'

Zafar heard her mutter in the distance as he tried to loosen his throat. He sank down onto his haunches and put one hand on the wall to give himself more blood to his head. With his other he loosened his collar.

The lift was suddenly the cabin of the private jet. His family would die from gunshots in a few spiralling seconds and there was not a thing he could do about it. So now it was his destiny to die. It was almost a relief. And he'd complained about being in line for the throne.

Distantly he realised she'd picked up the phone and spoken to the operator. When he heard her re-seat the instrument she bent down to him. 'You okay?'

He didn't refocus his eyes off the floor until he felt her hand on his arm - warm, firm, comfort personified – gripping him. He had the bizarre idea he couldn't fall anywhere while she held him. Yet all she did was share touch without moving. He breathed with difficulty through his nose and inhaled drifts of orange. Incredibly steadying like a shot of Valium through his bloodstream.

He sucked air through clenched teeth and the light- headedness faded. This was ridiculous. Irrational. Acutely embarrassing. He forced himself to look into her face.

The angel had dark golden eyes, like twisted treacle, calm and wise and filled with that compassion. Mesmerizing him up close. 'You're a nurse?'

Her eyes crinkled and his chest eased a little more. 'Sort of. I'm a midwife. Do you need some deep breathing?'

'I'm not in labour.' But this was hard work. He shut his eyes again. Tightness clenched him. 'Possibly.'

'Do you have a phobia?' The same gentle conversational voice as if she'd asked if he needed sugar in his tea.

The demons from the past battered against him. He strived to keep his voice level. 'So it appears.'

She sank down. He heard the rustle of fabric and felt the slight brush of her leg as she settled herself beside him on the floor. Her hand still rested on his arm, not moving, as if to transfer energy and calmness from her to him. It seemed to be working. 'What's your name?

He had many. 'Zafar.'

She paused and he felt her appraisal until he opened his eyes again. Her golden interest captured his. 'Well, Zafar. I'm Carmen. I've been stuck in this lift three times this week. Big, deep breaths should help.'

Deep breaths might be difficult. 'It is a battle with small ones.'

Coaxing. 'You can do a couple.'

He wasn't sure but the fact that she'd lived through this three times did help. He was feeling faint again. 'A rule of threes?'

'In through your nose...'

Intolerably bossy woman. '...out through my mouth. Yes, I know.'

Her voice firmed. Like his mother's from the distant past. The time of orange trees. 'Then do it.'

He humoured her. And felt better. Actually, quite a lot better, so he did it again. With her sitting below him, if he slitted his eyes open, he had a delightful view down the valley between her breasts. He glanced away politely but could feel himself improve every second with that picture in his mind. Surely a harmless medicinal remedy.

Imagine if the lift had still been full. He mentally shuddered. There was only her to see this weakness. Thankfully he'd sent his bodyguard and secretary to the suite. In future the stairs would be good for his fitness. Hopefully, once free, he'd never see this woman again.

A good thing for anonymity of weakness but a loss of something indefinable.

Her unexpected lushness drew him but he wasn't going to look there again. His gaze lifted to her face and a delightful mouth...those lips. His body stirred. A mouth designed for decadence and plump for surrender if he'd been willing to risk life and limb for it.

She may project calm but she looked very capable of protecting herself despite the weariness. Good to know. He wanted her safe. Which was odd that he cared.

'Are you feeling better?'

'Much.' Better than she knew. He watched with some amusement as she realised her neckline gaped and she stared straight back at him and raised her brows.

She removed her hand from his arm and shook her head. 'Tsk, tsk.'

The lift jerked and resumed its ascent. Zafar closed his eyes briefly but the panic had gone. Fled. Fixed elsewhere.

It seemed she was very good at her job. He straightened until he stood with his feet firm beneath him, reached down and took her hand to help her up. Such a lovely hand, but work worn. She rose fluidly, into his space as he'd intended. Ended nose to nose.

For that moment as their glances met he forgot the lift, the heights, the strain in his life, all except this unexpected awareness between two strangers swept away from their surroundings. He, so enmeshed in this unexpected connection, that when he said, 'Thank you,' the words were soft, gentle, and hung in the air like mist. Swirling around them.

An imp of mischief drew his head closer into her space. He expected her to pull away. 'You're very kind... and incredibly beautiful.' He lifted his hand to cup her cheek. Soft, soft skin.

She did the unpredicted. 'It's okay. I understand. Phobia.' He heard it – an underlying sympathy that horrified him. Pity?

He recoiled. He needed no one's compassion.

The elevator jolted and the doors opened on seven. They'd missed six altogether. She turned away from him with a frown.

There was some consolation in the way she compressed her lips together as if to hide the way they'd plumped and reddened in antici pation...of what? The almost brush of his lips on hers? Had she been tempted by that moment too?

'You certainly look better.' Her comment made him smile again, the dryness hiding undertones he couldn't pick but her cheeks glowed a deeper shade of red and her wide eyes searched his face as if confused by what had passed between them during the last few frozen moments.

Despite his urge to throw himself out of the lift to safety, Zafar stretched his hand across the doors to allow her to precede him. 'My apologies for my weakness earlier.'

She assessed him, a clinical scrutiny he wasn't used to from a woman. She strangled back a half laugh. 'I doubt you're a weak man so I'm sure you've good reason.'

He inclined his head.

She glanced around. 'And I should have got out at level six.' She scooted away from him and opened the door of the fire escape before he was fully out of the lift.

Her curvy bottom disappeared around the door like a promise. He let out his first normally composed breath. The day was not as bad as it had started out.

CHAPTER TWO – Carmen

Carmen walked swiftly away but she could still feel the eyes of the man in the elevator.

What had just happened? Her lips tingled as if still waiting and she could detect the unusual spicy aftershave from his skin so close to hers. And what a mouth! Wicked was too tame a word. Sinful maybe. Certainly seductive. She couldn't pretend she hadn't been tempted.

Not the sort of encounter she'd expected today and she wasn't entirely sure she'd behaved properly. Hopefully she wouldn't see him again.

When the fire escape door shut with an echoing clang she allowed herself a few seconds pause to breathe a sigh of relief as she leaned against it. Cold metal against her back dampened the heat everywhere else in her body. She glanced around.

Appropriate name. Fire escape. A fire to escape from.

She definitely felt a bit singed on the edges, like a ragged sleeve too close to a candle, smouldering and smoked. She touched her lips. Burnt and hot without even touching him.

She glanced around again, strangely reassured by a dark stairwell with unpainted concrete stairs and the echo of empty walls, glad of the sanctuary afforded.

One would have thought she'd learnt a lesson from her smooth-talking ex, that handsome men in expensive suits could seduce and destroy your life.

Still. One almost-slip didn't make a disaster. She hoped.

Eighteen hours later Carmen O'Shannessy admired the gifts Mother Nature had bestowed on her at five this morning with a soft smile. She knew there was a reason she loved night duty, apart from the fact it allowed her to work two jobs.

Twins. Dark-haired cherubs with skin like dusky rosebuds. Her patient, Fadia Smith, rested back in the armchair like Madonna with her sons poking out under her arms like tiny, bundled wings. It had taken a careful juggling, a few attempts, and almost an hour of patience but with both boys feeding well this moment was such a satisfying end to a drama filled morning.

It had been a long time since Carmen had seen twins born with so little fuss but then Fadia hadn't left them with much choice. Her cumbersome arrival alone and a bare five minutes before her first son appeared left Carmen literally catching the baby.

By the time the obstetrician and his entourage arrived, number two had also decided to greet the outside world and Dr Bennett had waved her on with an incredulous smile. To continue their no fuss arrival both wee boys had cried and then settled on their mother's skin and while they appeared small there were no signs of prematurity or respiratory distress.

That would be unlike the breathless-from-running neonatal staff who'd drifted back to their unit unneeded shortly after. Carmen still smiled over their shock when she'd rung for help.

Two hours later Carmen should've been feeling ready to hand Fadia over to the day staff and go home. Something niggled. 'You sure I can't phone someone for you?'

On cue with the question Fadia flinched in the chair and the two babies stopped their sucking with startled eyes before resettling to their feed.

To Carmen's eyes, Fadia seemed to force herself to relax. 'No, no. My babies are fine. I really don't have anyone else to call. I'm a widow and there's just a friend of my husband who's been helping me until my relatives arrive.' The hint of sorrow and melancholy hung around her.

Carmen wanted to hug her. 'If, you're sure?'

Fadia straightened, as if determined to show nothing was wrong and hurried on. 'We're all safe.' It seemed a strange thing to say.

'Well, your boys weren't waiting for anyone.' Carmen leaned over and stroked a tiny hand that rested on his mother's neck. 'You're amazing, Fadia. Congratulations. Tilly will be looking after you today. I going home to bed but I'll see you when you move to the Baby Hotel in a day or two. Have you decided on names?'

'Harrison and Braxton. My husband's names.'

'Lovely. I'm sure he would have loved that.'

'He didn't even know I was pregnant when he was killed.'

Was killed? Not died. How horrible but not the time to ask. 'I'm so sorry. But I'm sure, somewhere, he knows how wonderful you all are. Do try and get some sleep as soon as they rest.'

'Thank you, Carmen. You have shared much strength in this. Not cross at me for leaving it so late.'

'We all know babies come when they want. You had your own strength, Fadia. So amazing.' Carmen grinned. 'You must have a guardian angel and that make sense with your husband watching over you. Thank you for a lovely end to my night duty.' She almost bumped into Tilly, the day midwife, passing the door.

'Finally going home?' Tilly glanced at her watch.

Carmen saw she was nearly an hour late getting away already. 'At last.'

'You working this afternoon as well?'

'Doing the one pm at the hotel 'till seven. I'll rest now and then get to sleep in my bed tonight again.'

Tilly shook her head. 'Don't know how you do it. I'd be dead doing those hours as well as night duty.'

'I get four hours sleep.' Carmen shrugged. 'It's short term, but I'm starting to come down from the night's euphoria. Tired now.' She did not want to talk about this or the reasons. She was young. She could do it. She'd never taken help from anyone and she wasn't going to start now.

Thankfully Tilly wasn't slow on nuances because she changed the subject back to Fadia. 'Well done, you, with this morning. Lucky duck. Catching twins is hard to do without a cast of thousands trying to help these days.'

'And your Marcus didn't push me out of the way.'

Tilly's cheeks pinked and Carmen felt the tug of wistfulness at her friend's happiness. A fleeting picture of the man in the lift intruded again before she pushed him away.

She hadn't given him a thought for hours. Been far too busy. Which was a good thing. 'It must be great to have everything in your life going well.'

Tilly said, 'I'm fostering Marcus's faith in midwives. I think it's working. I love his ability to change.' They smiled at each other.

'And Fadia had no problems.' Carmen's smile dropped. 'Her friend's coming in at lunchtime. She's very quiet but then she did lose her husband recently. There's no one else listed as 'Next Of Kin' on her booking. Look after her, Till. We need to make sure she has somewhere to go after she's discharged.'

'Yes, Mother Carmen.' Tilly's answer was light but the look they exchanged reassured that her friend would be extra vigilant. Tilly would be just as determined as Carmen to be there for any mother, let alone one with twins who had twice as many reasons to need support.

After too few hours sleep it was time for Carmen to dress for work again. Postnatal midwifery in the Baby Hotel, a pet name the medical profession used for the five-star beach resort that catered for a few privately insured postnatal mothers.

Postnatal care was another warm and fuzzy part of her job and the women she supported often existed on less sleep than she'd had so a few yawns between friends was quite acceptable.

It was even better if she'd been with the women in labour and could follow their progress until they went home.

As she pressed the lift button in the car park she couldn't help thinking of the man on level seven. Zafar. Mysterious name. Mysterious panic attack. Yet, she was still glad she'd been there for him.

The memory of their close encounter burned bright.

She screwed up her face. 'Go away,' the words hung quietly between her and the closed elevator door and she twisted her head uneasily to make sure nobody had heard.

There'd been something incredibly vulnerable about such a virile and powerful looking man sweating over a stalled lift. Which could explain a little why she hadn't backed off more quickly.

Nothing vulnerable in the way he crowded her afterwards, though. Or the way she'd almost dared him to kiss her. She couldn't help the curve of her lips at the return of that memory and thought ruefully she'd bet he never wanted to see a woman who'd witnessed his phobia again.

Which was fine. Her husband's underhanded conniving had cost her the home she'd loved, undermined her self-respect – though she supposed she should thank him because she was tougher than ever now – and taught her to reserve judgement of good-looking men for a long while in the future.

But the lift-man's face seemed indelibly stamped in her memory. Dark tortured eyes under black brows and a firm yet wickedly sensual mouth. No doubt he captured her attention with his assurance – and a mouth that looked used to command...everywhere. She felt the re-kindling of awareness low and hot in her belly.

Outrageous thoughts. She shook her head. Don't even go there.

The guy embodied everything she hated about men. Power and prestige – she knew he had both despite his aversion to a stalled elevator, and she had no doubt he could be as cynically ruthless as he looked. Ruthless with women too, she bet.

Extreme wealth: of course. The watch, and the suit that shrieked of a tailor her ex would have killed to find, and they'd told her at reception he was in the Presidential Suite. So money in the realms of uncountable - though why he stayed out in the beach fringed east of Sydney was a mystery.

Back inside the lift she could picture him across from her easily...too easily in fact for someone she'd met for five minutes twenty-four hours ago.

The lift stopped on six and she stepped out onto the main baby floor and made her way to the midwife's room.

To work, Carmen!

At handover she was surprised to hear that Fadia had already moved to the hotel. Occasionally a very well woman with her second or subsequent baby would move across after four hours but for a first-time mum with twins it was very unusual.

'And the paediatrician said that was okay? And Tilly's Dr Bennett as well?'

'Neither were happy. But both will be visiting daily here they said, as well as the mothercraft nurse who transferred across with her.'

Special considerations, then. Not the first time a wealthy client had brought her own nurse but she hadn't envisaged Fadia like that. 'That will help.'

Her colleague shook her head. 'Not anymore. Fadia sent her away as soon as she was settled. Apparently didn't like her.'

'Not like the mothercraft nurse?' Carmen raised her eyebrows. 'Curiouser and curiouser.'

When Carmen knocked on Fadia's door a few minutes later, the last person she expected to open it was the man from the elevator.

Zafar.

Her pulse rate jumped and his eyes widened before he captured her gaze easily and held it, just as he held the small smile on his lips. Heat flooded her cheeks.

'Ah. The midwife. Come in.' As if she was always turning up on his doorstep.

She hoped her mouth was closed because, again, still, he looked jaw-droppingly handsome when he wasn't phobia'd out of his mind. He seemed ten times taller and broader than before but she guessed her first real impression must have been coloured by his distress.

'It seems I must thank you for your magnificent skills at the delivery of Fadia's twins.'

'Thank you.' Always be polite. 'Being there was a privilege. Fadia did all the hard work.'

He smiled sardonically. 'Yet some skill is required with multiple birth.'

He leaned casually against the door. Funny how she had the idea he was as nonchalent as a tiger about to spring.

Fadia, perched on the edge of the chair with one of her sons, looked anything but calm and Carmen's fluttery surprise turned to bristling protection of her patient.

Was the elevator almost-kisser the person Fadia had been scared of? 'Is this your husband's friend?'

Fadia shot a startled glance at Zafar and then back to Carmen's face. 'No. Goodness, no.'

Carmen couldn't help the relief. That saved a bad lack of profes-sionalism since she'd almost kissed him.

'No, this is my cousin. From Zandorro.' Fadia sent another glance his way, this time slightly less anxious. 'He's come in response to a letter I sent to my grandfather and to see if I need help.'

Zafar inclined his head. 'Ensuring you and your babies are well. Now also, to pass the good news onto your relatives, yes.' He turned to Carmen and raised one enquiring eyebrow. 'So, you, too, haven't met the illusive friend of our newest family members?'

'No.' And Carmen had no plan to elaborate. She shrugged to let him know that family dynamics were none of her business. 'But per-haps you could excuse us while I spend a short time privately with Fadia?'

'Is that totally necessary?' Such surprise when she'd said it and obviously a request uncommon in his experience. Carmen bit back her smile at his shock. So, we don't like being asked to leave, she thought. How interesting.

Just who was this man? Not that it mattered. She'd had four hours sleep, she was worried about Fadia, and wasn't in the mood for masculine tantrums. Face bland she said, 'Yes. Afraid so.'

Tough. Out you go. Though she didn't say it out loud.

He frowned down his haughty nose and thinned those sexy lips until they almost disappeared, which was a shame, but proclaimed this man expected obedience, not orders.

Carmen squared her shoulders and kept the smile on her face. My backyard, buddy. She could be as tough as he was. Or tougher if needed.

His eyes clashed with hers. It seemed he was going to cross his arms and flatly refuse. What would she do then?

She had no idea. Figure something out. Mentally she crossed her own arms. Bring it on. Never hassle a woman off night duty.

He didn't. On the brink of refusal, he hesitated and instead gave her a mocking smile that actually made her feel more uncomfortable than a flat refusal - almost a promise of retribution – and annoyingly her satisfaction at the win dimmed.

She didn't like that look. Or the feeling it left her with. Who was this guy?

'I shall return,' he said to his cousin with a stern glance in Carmen's direction, 'when your midwife is finished with you, Fadia.'

Fadia nodded, twisted her hands and Carmen inclined her head politely. She couldn't wait to ask Fadia what the problem was.

'We won't be long,' she said sweetly as she opened the door for him. The lock shut with the heavy finality of all good hotel doors and thankfully the room returned to a spacious suite.

Amazing how much breathing space one man could take up.

Carmen looked at her patient. 'You okay?'

'Yes.' The young girl hunched her shoulders and tightened her grip on the baby in her arms. Fadia didn't look okay. She looked shattered, on the brink of tears, and Carmen hurried across to touch her shoulder when really she wanted to hug her.

'And your babies?'

'Fine.' Fadia glanced across at her other baby asleep in the cot and visibly shook. 'I can't believe he actually left. You told him to go!'

'Of course.' She wasn't wasting time on him, she was worried about her patient. Something was badly wrong here.

'Zafar wasn't on your next of kin?'

'I didn't know if the family recognised me.'

'His arrival was unexpected?'

'Yes. No.' She lowered her voice. 'I wrote to my grandfather last week butHassan, my husband's friend, said I would be sorry when the family took over my life. But I'm glad Zafar is here while I decide what I wish to do.'

'Why is that?'

'I am safe if Zafar is here.'

Safe? What was going on here? 'Well, you have a few days to think about it before you have to go anywhere.' She took Fadia's pulse. It was faster than normal; she hoped just agitation, and not a postnatal problem. 'I'm surprised to see they allowed you out of hospital so soon after birth.'

'I could transfer to the hotel today as long as I brought the mothercraft nurse. My cousin visited me soon after you left this morning and arranged one when I asked.'

Carmen glanced around the otherwise empty room but didn't comment on the fact the mothercraft nurse was nowhere to be seen.

Fadia shrugged. 'We did not get on. She wished to take over. I dismissed her.'

'Oh.' Not a lot she could change there. 'Perhaps you could ask for another mothercraft nurse?'

'No.'

All righty then. 'You have had a rapid transfer for twins. Because of your over extended uterus you're at risk of bleeding; we need to watch for that. And get much more help if you stayed on the ward. I could have you readmitted there if you wish?' Especially if your cousin helped you leave too soon, she thought.

Fadia shook her head. 'Now that Zafar has found me,' she shrugged, 'I would prefer to be here. The doctors will visit me as well. I fear hospitals, hence my late arrival in labour. Zafar wished me to have a private nurse but we didn't suit.'

'You should try someone else.'

'I said I knew you and was comfortable without.' She looked up and pleaded, 'That is my biggest concern. I want to care for my babies myself not with nurse taking control as soon as they cry. Which is why I am unsure if I wish to return to Zandorro.'

Carmen wasn't so sure Fadia knew how much work two small babies could be. 'I can help while I'm here of course. It's a great way for a mother to feel. But it will be exhausting for you.'

The girl nodded with relief. 'Access to the Baby Hotel is why I chose your hospital. Tilly said you were working here today so I wanted to come across now.'

'Okay, I can understand preferring to be here than hospital.' But that didn't explain her cousin's agreement when most people would realise the twins needed more observation too.

'I do feel a little less alone now Prince Zafar has arrived.'

'*Prince* Zafar.' Carmen blinked. Prince of what? 'Like Prince Charles?'

'From the desert. Zafar is fourth in line to the throne of Zandorro.'

'A sheik then?'

Fadia nodded.

'So, you're from this Zandorro, too?'

'My family left when Zandorro was only a small but growing country in the desert. My parents are dead. My mother left five years ago and brought me with her. The royal family thought we had died so they left us alone.'

Carmen felt like a goldfish, stunned, with big eyes that looked out at the world, and her mouth open. A prince? *Gloop*. A sheik? *Gloop, gloop*. Drama, drama, drama.

She'd known he was someone out of the ordinary. Not your everyday occurrence to run into a prince. Or be trapped in a lift with one. Or be almost kissed by one.

No wonder he expected to be obeyed. And she'd coolly told him to leave. She struggled not to smile. Too funny.

She needed to think about this. 'He's your cousin?' Which made Fadia? 'So, you're a princess?'

'Yes.'

She pointed to the babies. 'They're princes, too, then? And you walked into the hospital at the very last minute, alone, to deliver twin princes?'

A cloud passed over Fadia's face and her voice lowered until Carmen strained to hear. 'Unfortunately, when my husband died, I was alone and pregnant and the only help I've had has been with friends of my husband's but I begin to fear I should not trust them.'

'I'm sorry to hear that. It must be distressing.' Carmen knew about loss of trust.

'Tom told me I was being followed and I moved out of my flat close to the hospital into a hotel for what turned out to be the last day of my pregnancy. The poor driver was beside himself that I would have my babies in his taxi.'

Carmen could imagine it. She'd bet he was terrified. Crikey. 'You're lucky they weren't.'

Fadia's eyes filled. 'I think Hassan didn't want Zafar to find me. He was angry. My uncle is here to take me back to his country. Now, I am beginning to think that is a good thing even if it separates me from my husband and mother who are buried here.'

She wiped away a tear. 'My sons need their heritage. Hassan said he will help me stay in Australia,' her voice became a whisper, 'but I'm not sure that is what I want.'

'This Hassan is your husband's friend? When is he coming, exactly?'

'Today sometime.' Her eyes filled with tears again. 'Suddenly I am uneasy about him seeing my sons.' Fadia began to twost her fingers and Carmen frowned as the girl struggled for composure. She fisted her hands. 'I hate being weak, but I seem to have lost my strength since my husband died.'

Poor Fadia. Just hours after birthing twins, And, oh my, she'd fallen into the middle of something here. Something intriguing as well as unsettling.

Then Harrison, the older of the twins, screwed up his face and let out a blood curdling wail as if aware of the disquiet in his mother. At least she could do something while her brain raced. She unwrapped the little boy and checked his nappy before she re-wrapped and lifted his scowling face out of the crib. 'Don't be cross, Prince Harrison.' Then she tucked him into her neck and gently patted his bottom. The unconscious rhythm soothed them both.

She needed to understand how she could help. 'So, tell me, Fadia. Do you want me to keep this Hassan away?'

Fadia's eyes widened. 'Can you do that?'

She inclined her head. 'Of course. Midwives are very good at screening people without upsetting them.' Carmen shrugged. 'Lots of times a mother's labour is not progressing because of an inappropriate person in the birthing room.' She grinned. 'Like a scary mother-in-law, or a friend she couldn't say no to. We suggest that person have some time out of the room and they don't return until the mother asks us to invite them back.' She spread her hands. 'I could hold Hassan off for you, but isn't your cousin better for that?'

Fadia stroked the bed sheet with her fingers. 'No. I am concerned the situation could escalate into danger.'

A strange thing to say but Fadia's fingers twisted and turned and Carmen held her tongue.

'Or Zafar might do something to him.'

Carmen barely stopped herself from rolling her eyes. Oh, come on. 'This isn't the middle ages.'

'You don't understand.'

'True, so help me to understand. This Hassan? Do you have a photo of him?'

Fadia thought for a moment and then nodded. She reached for her purse and removed a photo of a smiling couple. The woman was Fadia.

'Your husband?'

Fadia nodded and chewed her lip fiercely as if determined not to cry.

Carmen looked at the third person in the photo and yep, there was something about him that reminded her of her ex. Carl. Oh yes. A hardness around his eyes, a sleeziness in his smile. She was good at picking them now.

Fadia's fingers shook and Carmen touched her hand gently to still them. Enough emotional drama for this exhausted mum. 'Can I borrow this? I'll copy it and give my friend downstairs a copy. We'll keep an eye out and sort it so nobody will be hurt.'

Fadia's worried eyes stared at her, indecision clear.

'No rush for now.' Carmen held the baby towards his mother. 'Harry's going to bring the roof down if he really gets going. You're not going to have time to worry about annoyingHassans or frowning Zafars, because these boys will keep you on your toes without them.'

Fadia attempted a smile and some of the strain left her face. 'You're right. Thank you.'

'And after that you get to rest.'

They became immersed in the babies. Fadia smiled again at the expression on little Harry's face as he glared at her, and Carmen changed Braxton who dozed through it all, until mother and babies were serene again.

An hour later, when Carmen opened the door of Fadia's room, a tall man in a flowing white robe stood up from the chair at the end of the corridor and stared at her as she hesitated in the doorway. What was going on here?

Good grief. She shook her head – this was too crazy. She was guessing Zafar, the elevator prince, had put a guard on Fadia. Maybe there was more she needed to know.

They were infecting her with their dramas but the last thing the new mum needed was more tension and Carmen needed to know what she was up against.

Carmen stiffened her shoulders, let the room door shut behind her, and marched up to the guard. 'I'm assuming you're Prince Zafar's man?'

He bowed his head, though his expression remained anything but subservient. 'Yes, Madame. I am Yusuf.'

'Then, Yusuf, perhaps you could take me to your prince, please.'

'No.'

'No?'

'I think not.' The guard raised his eyebrows, looked her up and down, as if to say you are only a woman and a servant at that, and Carmen's usually placid temper flickered. She glared at him. Beyond a joke.

Any minute now Fadia could poke her head out and see she was under guard.

Her voice firmed. 'I think so. Right now, thank you. I'm quite happy to use the stairs.' She smiled sweetly. 'The Prince and I do know each other.'

A white lie. Serve Zafar right for flirting with her.

She and Yusuf – her new best friend…not – stared at each other for a moment and she could see a faint scar running the full length of the man's face. He was probably extremely useful in defending his Prince.

Stalemate as the silence lumbered on and she threw caution to the winds. 'I'd hate to have to pass on my displeasure.'

The man's face tightened and he shrugged fatalistically. 'As you wish. This way.' He opened the door to the stairwell and allowed her to precede him. Carmen could hear the swish of his robes behind her even though his footsteps were silent.

'Please wait.'

She glanced back and Yusuf held up his hand.

She paused at the top of the stairs and the guard leaned forward and opened the heavy door for her. That second of waiting gave her time to realise she had no clear agenda for her visit with the 'Prince' when she arrived. Was it enough of her business to barge in? What on earth was she doing here?

On the seventh floor Carmen could see another guard standing outside the door to the Presidential Suite and reality sank in a little deeper. How different this man's life was to hers. And, oh my how out of her depth she really was.

She paused to say she'd changed her mind but one glance at the cynical face beside her told her dear Yusuf had picked up on her discomfort. Great to know she was providing him with amusement.

That decided her.

Yusuf glanced once more at her determined chin, nodded at the man standing guard, then knocked on the large wooden door.

A few seconds later a tiny, white robed woman appeared and they conversed quietly in a language Carmen didn't understand but it wasn't hard to guess what was said - something along the lines of stupid woman annoying our prince, no doubt.

The woman glanced over Carmen, shrugged, and stepped back to allow them to enter.

The room opened into a window-lined terrace and the magnificent blue vista of Coogee Bay curved like a sickle seven floors below. The scent of sandalwood hung strongly in the air and in the background quiet discordant music played discretely.

Several low armchairs were grouped together as well as heaped cushions on vibrant green and gold carpets that Carmen suspected did not belong to the hotel. Most of the seating faced the entertainment centre on one side of the room and a boardroom table with a dozen comfortable chairs took up space on the other.

She'd been in this room before and the furnishing had changed dramatically. It seemed Prince Zafar travelled with a removalist van. A tad different to her bedsit with its rickety bed.

A door leading from another room opened and Zafar strode out. No, she thought, he did so much more than that. Dressed in the white traditional robes of a desert prince, with his head covered, he made quite an entrance. She couldn't help her mouth dropping open just a little.

His brows drew together when he saw her, but he came forward until he stood in front of her. Broader, and more formidable surrounded by his servants, but this time it was not only his physical presence, more the absolute mantle of distinct power.

'Is Fadia well?'

'Quite well.' She felt the pressure from interested eyes, and he too glanced around. He spoke three short sharp words that cleared the room like magic.

Despite herself she was impressed and couldn't deny a little nervous thrill now that they were alone. That was irritating. But not relevant to this conversation.

'Please—' he waved a hand to the lounge chairs '—be seated.' He gestured to the tiny butler's pantry. 'Would you like a juice or water?'

'No, thank you.' Despite her dry mouth. Maybe she should have taken a drink to give herself time to think of something to say.

He sat when she did. 'In that case what can I do for you, Miss Carmen?'

She had no idea. 'I wish to discuss your cousin.'

He inclined his head and she suspected a fleeting crinkle of amusement before he assumed a serious face again. 'I had guessed that was the case.'

Now she felt silly. She wasn't here because he'd almost kissed her. Was she? The thought brought a tide of pink to her cheeks and she felt like sliding under the gorgeous carpet or pulling one of those cushions over her face. How did she get herself into these situations?

Another flash of humour. 'Let me help you.'

She blinked. Not where she expected help to come from, but she'd take it.

'You're wondering if I am an ogre, or some medieval lord who drags unwilling women and their babies—' he caught her eye and she was sure he could read her agreement in her face, but he went on, '—back to being imprisoned in their homeland.'

Well she was making sure it wasn't something like that. 'Not quite so dramatic but yes.'

'Thank you for your honesty. Let me explain. Apart from things you cannot be aware of, I think to clear the air between us could save us both some time.'

He smiled at her, his teeth white and his lips curved, in a smile that made every bone in her body soften. She even leant slightly towards him until she realised what she was doing.

Stop it. Yet he did seem so reasonable and she was starting to believe she'd done the right thing to come here in the first place. This guy had serious charisma when he turned it on. That was a tiny worry. She needed to remember he could turn it on and off.

A random worry niggled and jostled with her sex hormones for attention. Please don't let me fall into idiosy again. Carl had been this smooth. This 'open' and friendly at first. Before she'd agreed to marry him and discovered how dark and dep his soul really sank. Too easily sucked in by smooth guys. That was her. Guys she almost allowed to kiss her in elevators.

She felt her shoulders stiffen with the thought. Good.

'By now you have discovered who I am although I imagine my title would mean little to you?'

The inflection made it a question and she answered like the puppet she was trying not to turn into. 'You're right. No idea.'

He smiled at her and there was no way she couldn't smile back, damn him. 'I am from the small state of Zandorro that has by the blessing of Allah found itself abundantly supplied with oil and precious gems.'

There seemed to be a lot of those around, Carmen thought cynically, but she nodded to show she was paying attention.

'Our grandfather, King Fahed Al Zamid is ruler, though his health is not good. Fadia's father, my uncle, was second in line to the throne until he died.' He looked at her. 'Of unnatural causes.'

Unnatural causes. She fought to keep her eyebrows level. He went on when she nodded. 'It was thought Fadia had passed away with her mother several years ago and as the succession passes only to a male child her wellbeing unfortunately slipped beneath the family's radar.'

An interesting way of putting it, Carmen thought but didn't say.

'My eldest brother is next in line,' he continued, 'and I too have become closer to the throne because of these misfortunes.'

He paused, a short one, to see if she understood and she was glad of the respite while she filed the order away in her brain. And came to the logical conclusion. 'Fadia's babies.'

'Indeed. Being male and healthy, they are next in line to succession not my brother or I.'

Next in line? To rule this small but extremely wealthy nation? Holy moly. Her mouth may have dropped open again.

'Unfortunately, this also increases their jeopardy from certain elements once their birth is known, and that is something I have tragic personal experience of. Naturally I am concerned that my cousin and her sons remain safe. And asked for my help.'

He'd said remain safe. Fadia had said safe. 'Safe? Do you mean from physical danger...like kidnapping?' This was somewhat more complicated than Fadia had led her to believe. If she believed him, that was, a calm inner voice suggested. Perhaps he was leading her astray with his talk of risk and safety and unsavoury elements.

'At best,' Zafar answered in a reasonable tone that seemed to flow hypnotically. 'Hence my urgency to find Fadia, once we knew she was alive. We wished to return her to our country before their birth in case all were endangered away from the palace. At least until we can address those who target my family once and for all. A goal I have been working on.'

'Do you think there is a risk of real danger?' She couldn't help thinking about Fadia's concerns of Tom.

'Certainly. Her eldest son is next in line to rule when he comes of age and the younger brother is the next in line again. Fadia's sons could provide leverage over the monarchy which unfortunately is not an uncommon occurrence with our hostile neighbours.'

She was starting to understand. Or perhaps to believe him. 'What will you do? You're not in Zandorro now.'

He shrugged philosophically. 'Fadia needs to come home, at least for the time being, for her and her sons' safety. Especially now she is a widow.'

'That won't be easy for her. I think she has some friends and a life in Australia.'

His lip curled. 'The friendship of a man who has plans to control a royal widow? A man who pretended to be a friend of her husband, who has helped her remain cut off from her family now she has no husband to protect her?'

So he knew a little about the illusiveHassan. Okay.

He asked quietly, 'What sort of man preys on a young woman like that?'

Indeed. But wasn't it Fadia's final decision? She stamped down her initial unease. 'She seems to have relied on him in the past.'

His gaze sharpened and she could almost smell the briny scent of storm to come. 'She has spoken of this man to you?'

'Not exactly.' She looked away. She really didn't think she'd get away with her pitifully thin denial but he wasn't looking at her. He'd focussed across the room at the windows. A pensive frown hardened his features.

'But has he already found where she is?'

She wasn't touching that assumption. 'Is that why you have a guard in her corridor?'

His gaze returned to her but he ignored her question. 'Fadia's marriage and the birth of her sons has been an unexpected development for our family. She must come home.' Carmen recognised implacable intent. On his face. In his voice. 'But even I would not whisk a new mother with twins away before she has had a chance to recover.'

'And when she has recovered enough to travel? Will you force her to travel home, even if she doesn't want that? Is that your intention?' She could see it was.

His look measured her. 'Yes.' There was no doubt in his mind anyway.

Now they were down to the real thing. 'Even if she's not a hundred percent she wants to go?'

'I believe it is in her best interest, and the best interest of her babies to return to Zandorro.'

'You wish to control her, then.'

'I wish to keep her safe.'

'And Fadia's wishes are not in the equation at all.'

Silence. She waited. 'You didn't answer my question.'

He rested his hands on the arms of the ornate chair. Met her gaze coolly. 'Again, you do not understand. It is my prerogative to not answer any question.'

'I see. Then until Fadia decides where she wants to take her sons she has my support. If she needs support.' Against you, but she didn't say it. She didn't have to. By the narrowing of his eyes he saw.

She stood up and he did also. 'I understand.' And she did, all too clearly. Her voice dry, she said, 'Thank you for seeing me.'

He studied her intently and she felt he could see not just her but right through her. Into her thoughts. Her conclusions.

It wasn't a comfortable feeling.

He said, 'I found our conversation to have been most illuminating.'

Because now he knew she was fully on Fadia's side? Had she given away something she shouldn't have. She didn't think she had. 'Yes. I've learned a little, as well.' Stew on that.

'Good day, Miss Carmen.' He bowed in a formal, old-fashioned manner and a small smile teased at the side of his mouth as if he found her amusing.

The air in the room grew cloying, the music dimmed, and his eyes burned into hers. She knew he was thinking of that moment in the elevator. She could feel the flush of heat sear her skin and yet she couldn't look away. His perusal drifted down and swept the full length of her. And it was as if he'd trailed a feather down her skin. She shivered and his eyes darkened even more.

She needed to get away. 'Good day, Prince Zafar.'

'My word it is, Miss Carmen.'

CHAPTER THREE
– Zafar

Zafar accompanied her to the door and watched her walk away up the corridor. Actually couldn't take his eyes off the proud set of her shoulders, the satiny swoosh of her hair, even toyed with the idea of calling her back, until he realised what he was doing.

Her shapely legs would show to advantage in shoes other than the flat brogues and her formless tunic still did not disguise the lushness of her body. He could quite clearly remember yesterday and had welcomed the scent of her skin next to his today.

Unexpected recognition when he barely remembered any woman since his life had been torn apart by the loss of his family. The memory saddened and pulled his mind away from Fadia's midwife.

Poor, sweet Adele. Theirs had been an arranged marriage, she so much younger than him, eager to please and expecting her husband to keep her safe. Her broken-hearted family had entrusted him with their precious daughter and he had failed them all.

Still the burden of that guilt weighed heavily on him, the picture of her frightened eyes before the gunman opened fire haunted him in his sleep.

He hadn't looked at another woman since. Had lost himself in his work until recalled to royal duty. Now his task was to ensure Fadia and her sons were safe. Nothing else mattered. But he feared it would not be easy.

That was his real problem. He feared. Feared he would not be able to stop something terrible happening. Unable to save Fadia and her sons like he had been unable to save his own family.

Prior to two years ago he'd been afraid of nothing. Nothing. Until evil had arrived. He would not rest until it was conquered. He would not be distracted.

His eyes strayed to the empty corridor. Perhaps the midwife could help. And so his deliberations returned to Carmen as he turned thoughtfully back into his suite.

She had braved the lion in his own den. He admired her courage. And she amused him with her determination not to be cowed by his prestige.

But she had lied about knowing nothing of Fadia's friend.

The dog might be here in the hotel. He would have Yusuf investigate. And delve into the delightful Miss Carmen's past too. Perhaps she could help his cousin more than they knew and such information would be useful.

He needed Fadia and the twins well enough to travel as soon as possible. He would feel better when he had them back in Zandorro, where their security could be controlled.

Zafar strode across the room and out the doors onto the balcony, punished himself with the rise of gall in his throat from so small a height, he forced himself to grip the rail and glance below. His gut rolled and he stepped back as he drew breath.

Back against the wall, his spine pushed hard into the unyielding stone, his mind roamed while he stared out over the rolling sea.

Carmen's words in his memory. Breathe. In and out. Calm returned. If he cut off the bustling town below, the ocean seemed not dissimilar to the rolling dunes of his desert.

Breathe.

He could feel a lightening of his mood that normally only came when he retreated to solitude.

A whimsical thought intruded where none normally went. He wondered what Miss Carmen would think of the desert or the ways of a desert prince. It was an unexpected but intriguing scenario.

CHAPTER FOUR –
Carmen

Carmen clanged the door behind her as she left the Presidential Suite. Her favourite place. The fire escape.

He'd burnt her again.

It was criminal to be that handsome and mesmerising. But at least she'd found out that Fadia was simply a pawn on his gold embossed chess set, and she, Carmen O'Shannessy, didn't like the idea. Or him. If Fadia needed an ally then Carmen was her girl.

It brought back too many unpleasant memories. The way Carl had turned, as early as their honeymoon, swearing at her, keeping her awake with tirades when she needed to sleep, wearing her down, demeaning her after a year of desolation until she finally accepted the enormity of her mistake and ran away. Moved jobs, states, losing friends until finally she rebuilt her life.

Domineering men did not have a place in her life. She straightened off the door and began her descent. Unfortunately, she could picture

Zafar's wicked smile so easily and the warmth she'd felt when he turned it her way.

No. No trust especially for men who could cool and heat her body with just a glance. So why did she want to run back and relive the sensation? How did that work?

When Carmen opened the door on the sixth floor, of course her friend the guard sat there. He stood from his chair when she appeared and nodded coldly as she walked past him towards her own room at the end of the corridor.

Made a good little enemy there, she thought, as she stared past him to the rooms of mums and babies that looked out over the beach. When she reached the end of the corridor the Midwife's Room welcomed her with sanctuary from his beady eyes.

Didn't matter if her room held only spare supplies. At least she could shut the door - which she did firmly - and lean back against it.

Unfortunately, the barrier didn't help her brain.

Carmen pushed herself off the door and straightened the empty baby cots before energetically restocking the linen from the trolley into her shelves. Still needing distraction she wiped over the bath equipment and scales she used to weigh the babies.

'Done. Hmm.' She rested her hand on her computer at the desk, but she didn't see any of it. She could see Prince Zafar, though, in her mind's eye, and he was smiling...

Not fair.

On Tuesday, refreshed after a full night's sleep, back at the baby hotel Carmen welcomed the new mothers freshly arrived from their birth at the nearby hospital.

It took at least half an hour for each new mother to be ensconced and resting. When she finally made it to her room the phone shrilled, as if it were impatient with the neglect.

'Midwife. Can I help you?'

'Carmen? It is Fadia. I have been trying to phone you for ages. There's a pink rash on Harrison's leg that is new. I need you.'

She'd seen Fadia when she first came on duty but hadn't stayed long. 'I'll come very soon. Everything else is okay?' No word from Hassan she hoped.

'The boys and I are fine, otherwise, if that's what you mean?'

Carmen relaxed. She just had this feeling of disquiet she couldn't explain. 'Is it okay if I check on one of my other mothers first?'

'Oh?'

A little of the privilege she was used to had crept into Fadia's voice. Interesting family. Carmen smiled into the phone. 'I'll be as quick as I can but might be ten minutes or so. That way I can spend longer with you when I get there.'

'Of course. I understand. I'll see you soon.'

The time Carmen spent with the other young mum seemed to fly and she glanced at her watch as she waved goodbye.

She needed to arrange times for weights for those who were going home that day, but she'd better check the princess first. She made her way to Fadia's room. With two babies to care for she needed the most help.

Carmen knocked, then opened the door with her key, and she almost walked into Zafar who again was with his cousin.

His black brows rose in disbelief. 'You have a key?'

Carmen shared her own frown. That tone. That arrogance. She wasn't sure why it goaded her so much but thankfully she wasn't one of his underlings. 'Yes. To all the mother's rooms so they don't have to get up to let me in.' She tilted her head at him. 'I always knock first. Do you?'

He didn't answer. Instead, inscrutable, he said, 'I'm sure you do,' which left Carmen seething. What was it about this man that pressed her buttons? Normally the most easy-going person, just a glance from him was enough to raise her blood pressure, and yet his actions were reasonable in the circumstances.

Why wasn't her response more tranquil?

She narrowed her eyes at him. Did he think she was in collusion withHassan? Or whomever else he considered to be hostile dangers to his cousin? 'Do you come often? I hope Fadia is able to rest between feeds.'

'My cousin would be able to rest if the midwife came immediately when she was asked.'

Snippy. Tsk, tsk. Real world. 'As it happens, your cousin is not my only patient.'

His lips tightened and he glanced at his watch. 'Then I will arrange for it to be so.'

There it was. Yup. Red rag to her bull. 'You will do no such thing, Prince Zafar.'

She stressed the title, more to calm her own urge to throttle him, than in respect. Was this guy for real? The most annoying part being she couldn't let her feelings show because drama was the last thing Fadia needed. She smiled at her patient before she turned back to the royal pain.

'Perhaps this topic is best saved for a time that isn't taking up your cousin's rest opportunities.' She moved past him. Brisk, businesslike, ready to do her job. 'Now, Fadia, would you like to show me your baby's rash?'

Zafar's voice floated over her shoulder. 'I have told her it is *erythema toxicarum* and that it is normal in the first three days in newborns.'

Carmen blinked but didn't turn to look at him. Obviously he had medical advantage he hadn't mentioned. Typical to keep her in the dark.

'Prince Zafar is a paediatrician and has established the new children's hospital in Zandorro before he was recalled to his duty to the monarchy.'

Which would explain his knowledge and also why they'd let the twins out so early. Der. They had their own paediatrician. She looked at the red pimply rash on Harrison's neck and arms. Okay. Correct diagnosis.

'He's right.' She smiled at Fadia. Not at him. 'You might find that the rash moves with heat. Meaning, if you were to hold Harrison's leg while you changed a nappy you might find the rash had suddenly become more prominent there and less prominent where it showed a minute ago.'

Zafar stepped closer. 'I agree Fadia looks tired. Is there a nursery where the babies can go while she sleeps?' Apparently His High and Mightiness was over harmless rashes.

'I'm afraid we don't have that option here.' And who had made it easier for her to leave the hospital ward too quickly, Carmen thought? Hmm. 'This facility is for transition to home. If Fadia wants to have the babies minded, she could return to the hospital or have a relative stay in the room while she rests?'

She spread her hands. Her look said she doubted Fadia would relax while he was watching over her.

'Or I could hire a mothercraft nurse, again. Surely that would be easier?' Zafar queried his cousin but Fadia's eyes pleaded as she shook her head. 'No. Please.'

Zafar frowned and Carmen wondered if he regretted hurrying her here. She hoped so. She watched his face but nothing showed. Typical. Well, Fadia needed rest. And it would be better if her left.

'For the moment we will do as you wish.' He turned and headed for the door before she could ask him to go. 'I will discuss this with your midwife later today.'

And when would that be? To worry about later. For the moment Carmen was pleased she didn't have to fight about asking him to leave.

Left to their own devices the women had babies fed and settled within the hour, despite a tantrum from Harry that rattled the windows, and an inclination from Braxton to sleep though the feed. Finally the curtains closed so Fadia could rest.

'Please ring me if they wake and you need help to get sorted for the feed.'

Fadia nodded sleepily.

'Leave a voice message if you get stuck. If I get tied up, the other midwife will be here, soon. In which case I'll see you tomorrow.'

Fadia yawned and smiled sleepily and Carmen let herself out. She still had three more mums to check.

The day seemed to stretch forever but tonight was the second of the four in her week when she could fall into bed and sleep the night through.

As seven o'clock drew closer she found herself looking forward to finishing. Handover took longer than normal for the night midwife because the intricacies of Fadia's case involved gentle handling of the confidential aspects of royalty and awareness of the new danger aspect. Finally, she was riding down in the lift to the basement on her way home but she felt so wired she worried she'd just toss and turn in her bed.

When she stepped out below ground a deep voice commented, 'Good evening, Carmen. You look fatigued.'

Zafar leant up against her car. Was that a coincidence or did he really know it was her vehicle? Weariness suddenly took a back seat to nervous energy. 'I'm feeling a little jittery after my long day today. Don't cross me.'

He smiled, unperturbed, but offered no explanation as he watched her. Dark eyes, Amused mouth. Broad shoulders leaning.

She tapped her foot. Irritability, not nervous energy, now. She wished he'd go away. Really. Honest. 'Did you want something, Prince Zafar? Apart from saying I look tired which was very kind. Thank you.'

Zafar pushed himself off her bonnet and loomed in front of her. 'I wish to invite you to walk with me. Even drained you are lovely.'

Yeah right. Lovely with little sleep. She resisted the urge to brush her hair back. A walk? 'Now? It's almost dark?' She narrowed her eyes. Kidnapping had been mentioned. 'Why?'

He shrugged. 'Because it would be good to get out of the hotel. Walk along the beach path. What is it you say? Blow away the cobwebs? That is one of the things I miss most about Australia. The graphic expressions.' He'd lived here before then.

She wished it hadn't been such an enormous twenty-four hours because his background and history couldn't help intrigue some part of her. Most of her, really.

Had he lived here before he was a prince? As a young doctor? That made him more normal. She met those every day.

The idea of walking in the fresh air before driving to her solitary flat tempted. Let the stresses of the day be whisked away into the salty breeze that blew a mere hundred meters away. It held appeal, as did the idea of hearing a more about this enigmatic man in front of her.

'Perhaps a short walk. I do sleep better with exercise.'

'Most obliging,' he mocked gently.

Carmen glanced at her car, shrugged her shoulders, and added, 'Or I could go home now?'

He smiled. And what a smile. The most spontaneous grin she'd seen. 'I am walking. Would you care to accompany me?'

It seemed she did want to go, because her legs made their own decision and followed him up the ramp, his request for company pulling her like a string.

The late afternoon light glowed golden as she stepped into it beside Zafar. Not long until sunset but the salty tang of ocean breeze reinforced her decision to get out into the world.

She didn't know what made her look back, in truth she'd forgotten about his bodyguard, but the man was there in the lee of the building watching them. His eyes met hers coldly and a shiver tickled her neck.

CHAPTER FIVE – Zafar

Zafar saw her frown and shiver – looked back at his man and with a flick of his wrist he banished Yusef from sight.

He wasn't sure why it had felt so important he wait and talk with this woman. This midwife. Carmen.

His brain had suggested he required a discussion of Fadia but his intent had shifted as soon as she stepped out of the lift. His mood rose and paranoia fell. How did she do that? Why? And how did he stop it happening? Because it was dangerous.

They waited at the traffic lights and strangely the silence lay lightly between them. His interest in the companionship of a woman had been absent for the last two years and yet her company made him feel bright and deceptively free.

'Exercise is something I miss when I'm busy with work,' she mused. Not looking at him. Said easily, as if he were a person she knew and didn't need to impress. She was unlike anyone he had met.

'Walking is good for the mind,' he agreed. 'And sea breezes such as this should carry weight away from the soul.'

She glanced at him. 'I like that.' Again, easily, and he felt himself relax further. 'The sea makes me feel calm.'

'Are you not always serene, Carmen,' he teased. 'I do not believe it.' Remembering the lift and her oasis of peace she'd shared during his anxiety. He admired her. Not an emotion he expected. Perhaps it was her genuine empathy he could feel for his cousin. Perhaps her obvious lack of ulterior motive? Or her transparent emotions that enticed him to savour her moods - even when he annoyed her.

She smiled. 'I have my storms and tempests like everyone else. Tell me about the desert. Fadia says your country has enormous areas of dunes.'

Yes, his land was an ocean of sand. 'The desert is my sea,' he said as the walk sign propelled them across the road and down to the cobbled walk that ran around the headland. 'It calms me like the water and waves calm you.'

'I've never been to the desert.'

'It is very beautiful and unforgiving.' He smiled down at her. What was it about her that captured his interest? Held his attention like a magnet. 'Like some Australian women appear.'

'Never mind. If Fadia is happy in her decisions I'll forgive you.'

'Will you?' He felt his mouth curve until he realised what he was doing. Flirting. He was not here for this. But he would like to see her pampered, cosseted, cared for like the women in his home. The worries of the world removed from her lovely shoulders. Perhaps one day, when he was not called to royal duty and all this was over, he might come back and search her out. See if she still wanted to see the desert.

It was an intriguing idea he shouldn't consider.

He put his hand on her elbow to steer her safely aside as a pushbike rider peddled past, going a little too fast on the narrow walkway. Her skin was like silk, yet taut with youth and vibrancy. He could feel the impact of her arm on his fingers.

Touching her skin should not be this distracting. Zafar let his hand drop. Too soft yet supple, too enticing and he had no right to touch her.

The guilt swamped him. How could he forget his wife so easily? Just two years and for the first time in so long he was burdened with the beginnings of lust? For a woman so different from his beloved.

So why did he want to capture this woman's hand and bump his hip against hers as they walked. Why now, suddenly, did he see Carmen as attractive when for the last eon he'd barely acknowledged other women existed?

What was it about her?

CHAPTER SIX – Carmen

Carmen tried to ignore the teasing and the excitement she could feel growing at his company. This was not good. They were worlds apart. But sharing space now was a temporary thing. She could enjoy her walk and satisfy her curiosity.

No strings attached. 'If you are a prince, do you have a palace?' A little tongue in cheek. He probably lived in a nice house in the city.

'Yes.'

She blinked and looked at him. He shrugged. 'My brother and I each have our own palace in the mountains and share service to our grandfather at his grand palace in Zene, the capital of Zandorro.'

Oh. That seemed too fairy tale but it made her feel more secure enjoying his company. A man this grand would not be interested in an ordinary midwife. He probably had a camp in the desert with servants and tents.

'There is also an oasis.' It was as if he read her mind.

'A Bedouin camp?'

'Certainly. You would not believe it.'

'Like Lawrence Of Arabia?' They smiled at each other. 'Tell me.'

He shrugged, looked amused. 'A true Bedouin camp is a little more earthy than mine. My oasis belonged to a tourist company who unfortunately spiralled into bankruptcy. I bought them out when I could have waited for them to leave but this way the karma is good.'

He guided her past a small dog that had stretched his lead across the path. 'I use it for business negotiation when western wives accompany their husbands. Their fantasies are excellent business. Bathing in oils, traditional dress for the meal. I think you might enjoy it.'

Instead of double shifts and sore feet? 'It could be fun.'

'I could help you enjoy it.'

'I'll bet.' But she wasn't worried. He was joking. 'Are you saying because I'm Australian I'm easily swayed by that fantasy?' She was having a few pretty pictures of her own. She smiled at him. 'I'm all for fantasies as long as I can get off the make-believe merry-go-round when I want to.'

She knew Zafar watched her face. Could probably see the dreamy expression in her eyes at the idea. But she wasn't a fool. Nothing was really as it seemed. 'Australia will always be my home.' She tilted to see his face. 'You said you've lived here before?'

He looked across at her as they walked past the old baths. 'My mother was buried in Sydney.'

'Did she leave Zandorro late in life?'

She waited for an answer. He looked lost for a moment and she wished she hadn't asked about his parents if it made him sad.

'Yes, my mother left Zandorro when my father died. She married an Australia diplomat a few years later.'

'My brother and I were left behind in our grandfather's care. It wasn't until I demanded to come to university here that I learned she'd had no choice if she wanted a life for herself.

Her face turned to him. 'I'm sorry. You must have missed her.'

'Yes.' So, he'd been in school. Too young to lose his mother. She hoped his grandfather had been kind but she suspected otherwise. 'Where did you live when you were here?'

'And why am I speaking of things I share with no–one?'

She smiled at him. 'Because you will leave soon and never see me again. And I'm genuinely interested.'

She couldn't read his expression. But felt his surprise at her answer. 'As you wish. I lived with my mother and her husband, all through my university studies. Bought a residence near theirs until I completed my time as registrar. That was three years ago.'

'You worked here as well? For a long time?' As a doctor?

'I studied under Dr Ting at Bay Hospital.'

CHAPTER SEVEN
– Carmen

D r Ting? Carmen sucked in a breath. 'You're a consultant?'

If he'd been under the eminent paediatrician then he was no slough. No amount of money would have secured the radical but brilliant Dr Ting's agreement unless Zafar was worthy.

She looked at him with new respect. 'I'm impressed.'

He frowned. 'Don't be. I've left the work I trained for. Unable to practice.' Such was the despair in his voice she backed away from the topic. This guy could create emotion in her with just a word and she wasn't used to that. More layers she didn't understand and more reasons to be careful.

The silence had a bite to it now. Something had happened to stop his work. She wondered but restrained her natural impulse to ask.

'Did you work at all in Zandorro?'

'I had two years. Returned with innovative ideas, bitten by my mentor's passion, obsessed with creating a better place for sick children. Even set up research facilities. Before my royal duties caught up with me. But enough of me.'

She got that. She changed the subject. Maybe too abruptly. 'The view is spectacular along this path.'

'Yes. It is.' The darkness in his tone made the water in front lose its sparkle. Such was his presence the idea didn't even seem too fanciful. Maybe night was just coming on more swiftly than she'd anticipated?

They walked briskly along the cliff past the steps to the Ladies Baths and onto the wide grassed area near the playground.

She noticed the families gathering blankets, children tucked under their arms, some squealing in protest and others too tired to care. They seemed in a hurry.

She turned curiously to survey the way they'd come.

A summer storm had gathered like a dark column behind them and she lifted her hand to point it out when she was distracted by a young woman in a pretty sarong kneeling on the grass.

At first Carmen thought she was praying until the woman moaned, an unmistakable guttural sound to a midwife's ears, and they both stopped. She turned her face and the woman's glittering, fear-filled eyes made Carmen draw breath as they both crossed the grass quickly to her side.

Carmel surveyed the scene. Alone and distressed. Like Fadia. Why are these pregnant women out and alone in labour?

Carmen rested her hand on her shoulder. 'What can we do to help you?'

The woman moistened her lips. 'An ambulance? My stomach.'

Around them the once-busy park now lay deserted as the cooler breeze of the impending storm sprang up. 'Are you in pain? Have your waters broken?'

The young woman reached out and squeezed Carmen's hand in a tight grip. 'Both.'

She turned her head and she too, realised they were the only people left. Her eyes avoided Zafir and sought Carmen's. 'I'm scared. It's like a freight train. The pains are slamming me. Don't leave.' The woman stopped and moaned as she tried to catch her breath.

'I won't. Ambulance, please, Zafar?' Carmen glanced at her companion, who nodded and raised his phone to make the call, as Carmen knelt down beside her. 'What's your name?'

'Jenny

'I'm Carmen, Jenny. And this is Zafar. Is this your first baby?'

The woman nodded. Carmen's shoulders relaxed a little. So hopefully they'd have time to transport. 'Can you stand? We've called an ambulance. Would you like to move to the bench?'

Jenny looked at the short distance to the sturdy steel bench. 'No. I don't think so. I'm too scared to move. I need to stay like this.'

Carmen's eyebrows lifted. She glanced at the roomy sarong – one of those tube ones held up by elastic – and decided the woman was probably as comfortable kneeling as she'd be anywhere.

At least she'd be covered for privacy. They could probably have a baby under that sarong and nobody would notice.

At work most of her births were in the semi-dark and by feel anyway, but it wouldn't come to that.

'That's fine. Your comfort's the most important thing while we wait for the ambulance.'

She exchanged glances with Zafar, a wordless request for support and he nodded. Good. She slid her hand over the woman's stomach and her belly lay rigid as a board beneath her fingers. 'The contractions are powerful.'

The girl nodded.

'You're breathing so well.'

'I did classes.'

'So you know it's important not to be scared.'

'I'm beyond scared. I'm freaking here.' Jenny ground the words out.

'I'm a midwife.' Carmen pressed her hand into Jenny's shoulder. 'You're doing great. Fear is your worst enemy. I try to remember that when things happen that scare the socks off me. Birth isn't an enemy, it's nature's way.'

Jenny shook her head. Emphatically. 'It shouldn't be this quick.'

'Sometimes that happens,' Zafar said quietly. Reasonably. 'Everything will be as it should if a little unusual in setting. Carmen is truly a midwife and I, a paediatrician. We know babies. Someone up there is looking after you.'

'And babies are spontaneous and pretty tough.' Carmen sent Zafar an ironic glance that said, hope you're ready for this. 'Do you want to slip off your underwear in case? Might be tricky otherwise.'

CHAPTER EIGHT –
Zafar

Zafar compressed his lips to hide his smile. The young woman was clearly terrified but Carmen had it all well in hand. He could only observe, uselessly, for the time being without interfering. He was afraid he couldn't achieve the same degree of calm she had with so little time.

But he was more than willing if there were complications with the newborn.

Jenny shook her head. 'I don't want to move.'

'And we can work with that if we have to.' Carmen tilted her head down lower so the woman could see her face.

'Are you pushing?'

'A little.'

'If your baby is born I'll catch and pop him or her through your legs to you at the front. Do you understand?'

The woman moaned and then a look of surprise and horror crossed her face. 'This can't be happening.' Her eyes darted around as if the ambulance would suddenly appear.

'It's about to happen.' Carmen looked to Zafar and he nodded. Yes, he'd back her up if needed, but this was not what he wished for. Where was the ambulance he'd called? They both knew an imminent birth when they heard one.

Serenely Carmen said, 'If it happens we'll lift your baby and put him or her against your skin under your dress and pop the head out of the neckline. The length of the umbilical cord will tell us how high to lift it. Okay?'

'Noooo,' Jenny wailed, then groaned as she suddenly scrambled to push her panties off

Carmen rolled the woman's underwear up neatly as it appeared from under the dress and Zafar decided that no doubt she had a use for that too.

He was reminded of her calmness in the lift and it was the same here.

As if she were saying, having a baby in the park is no big deal. She appeared so calmly focussed that even the woman looked as though things might be fine after all. A mindset that had seemed insurmountable a few moments ago.

Why wasn't he surprised?

He should really add something in reassurance but he was only a spectator – an appreciative one – unless his skills were required.

Skills he hadn't used enough lately. Very quietly he added. 'We'll be here for you and your baby until the ambulance comes.'

He copied Carmen's calm tone then stripped off his jacket and bundled it up like a pillow to keep the warmth inside for the baby when born. He had no doubt Carmen would manage most of the impending birth.

It had been several years since he'd seen a precipitous birth and not something he'd expected along a cliff path. He hoped this baby was well because he didn't fancy resuscitation out here in the freshening breeze but they would manage what they had to. The ambulance couldn't be too far away.

The woman groaned and he focussed back on the present. Carmen had shifted around behind Jenny, shielding her from the path and lifting her dress slightly. 'Head on view,' she murmured and held her hands either side of the baby's head. He wished he'd had gloves he could have given her but doubted she'd give it a thought in this moment.

The sound of the ambulance in the distance overlaid the sound of Jenny's breathing. All the while in the background the crash of the surf on the cliffs melded with the rumble of distant thunder, raising the expectation of drama about to be played which added to the surreal, amazing, incredible moment he hadn't anticipated.

'Here it comes,' Carmen said calmly, 'you're doing beautifully.'

Jenny moaned, the baby's head appeared, and then slowly the little face swivelled to face the mother's thigh. Seconds later a shoulder and then two arms eased into Carmen's hands in a tangle of limbs and cord and water and the baby gasped at the cold air on wet skin and cried loudly as his legs and feet slid out.

Zafar smiled at the swollen scrotum. A son. 'Hello there, young man.'

Then the memories rushed in. His own son. Limp and bloodless.

Zafar quickly wiped the baby over with the warm inner lining of his jacket to dry his damp skin and prevent chilling. Carmen eased baby between his mother's legs under the tube of material into her waiting hands.

Zafar listened to her soft voice as if from a distance. Shook his head to shut out the echoes from the past. His own joy at Samir's birth. The look between he and Adele at the moment of birth. The summit of their expectations. His family.

The family he lost. Both dead. Both buried.

The bleakness of loss washed over him until the newborn cried again and he shook himself back to the present. This was not his son. This baby cried vigorously and healthy and began his new life on a windswept headland.

'Oh, well done, Jenny.' Carmen's voice. It was over. Incredible.

'Nice long cord, that's handy,' she murmured.

Handy, he thought. Such a handy length of cord. And suddenly his mouth tilted, the painful memories receded and the miracle of new life made his lips curve into a smile he wouldn't have believed possible a moment ago.

Women amazed him – these two in particular – and the memory of the last ten minutes would no doubt make him smile for years to come.

Carmen glanced across at him, met his eyes with delight in hers, and his smile broadened. 'Very handy,' he agreed.

She frowned and then must have remembered what she'd said. *Handy cord.* She grinned back at him then down at the mother.

Within fifteen minutes the ambulance had transferred mother and baby to a stretcher and was ready to leave. Zafar was glad to see the officers offer towels and hand steriliser to Carmen who blithely washed herself down. His jacket had been bagged for washing because Carmen wouldn't let him put it in the waste.

'You could reminisce when you put that on,' she'd said. He doubted he'd wear it but she had a point. His mouth curved again.

Soon mother and baby were swathed in blankets in the back of the vehicle. Everyone happy with their condition, and with the air-conditioner set on warm, they closed the doors.

Zafar dropped his arm around Carmen's shoulder and pulled her body in next to his as they watched the flashing lights disappear.

She slid into the side of his body too well and he fought to keep the moment a platonic well-done, because for him, something had changed. Not just in the way he felt about this amazing woman but about the colour and promise of the future he'd thought would always be grey.

The idea of new life in unexpected places, perhaps even the easing of the pain he'd carried since that fateful hijacking two years ago when he lost so much, and now for the first time he felt hopeful.

He frowned. Because of Jenny's birth? An unknown woman's son? Or because of the midwife?

All he knew was he did owe some of this amazing feeling to this woman. And again, outside his usual experience, she genuinely didn't want anything in return for the blessings she'd bestowed on him.

'It's almost dark,' she said.

Zafar too, had noticed. 'Indeed. I fear we're in for a storm.'

'Good grief! Look at that.' While they'd been busy a new weather front had loomed apocalypse angry and not a slight summer storm.

The wall of cloud rolled like dark oil off a cliff, grey and black cumulous with angry faces that shape-shifted as they lit with lightning.

Zafar gestured her to precede him. 'I think we should return more quickly.'

'You think?' she muttered as she hurried along in front of him but it was far too late to reach the safety of the hotel.

He pulled her into the lee of a bull-nosed iron picnic shed as a sheet of cold rain blew across the path. Their legs were instantly splattered with pea-sized drops followed by a deafening crack of lighting exploded into the ground on the cliff edge. Carmen jumped and he tightened his arms around her. Felt her shudder beneath his hands. Quiver and quake under her skin.

Zafar loved storms but it seemed Carmen had her own phobias. At least he wasn't the only one with situational fears. 'Shh. We'll be fine here.' It seemed so long since he'd held a woman to comfort her, felt his chest expand with the need to protect, set his feet more firmly as if to ward off anything that would threaten her.

The briny scent of ozone seared his nostrils and two seconds later thunder directly overhead rattled the roof of their shed like a giant hand. It slammed their pitiful shelter with a noise and light.

CHAPTER NINE – Carmen

Carmen shuddered under Zafar's arms. His heat surrounded her, arms strong around her shoulders and instinctively she tucked her forehead into his chest. His shirt was fine but thin and she could feel the corded muscle solid beneath her cheek, warm and welcoming, and the steady thud of his heartbeat in her ear calmed her own.

The tickling spice of an exotic aftershave, one that made her think of souks and incense – and lifts – made her bury her nose deeper and banish the smell of rain and ozone with a big shuddering inhalation. It was just that she hated storms. She'd always been afraid of storms. Let alone this mighty storm.

'I hate thunder,' she mumbled shakily into his shirt when finally the ringing in her ears made talking possible. She ignored the tiny voice inside her that wondered if this time she told the whole truth.

He leant down and even the warmth of his breath calmed her as he spoke into her hair, 'We will stay until the lightning has passed.'

There was no sign he would loosen his embrace and she was quietly pleased about that. There was something primal about the extreme force of nature around them and she knew about the danger of reckless exposure. She should distract herself from the storm and think about Jenny and her new baby and how lucky she'd been to avoid this storm.

But she couldn't distract herself from the feel of Zafar's arms, a strength that kept the outside world at bay like a force field, a zone she was very happy to be safely within.

To her chagrin she snuggled deeper into the haven he afforded. 'Just let me know when you're ready to move,' she mumbled into his chest.

He shifted his mouth until his breath was warm in her ear again. 'I was thinking of making a move now.' He squeezed her arms with teasing pressure. His voice low and holding a distinct thread of humour she couldn't miss. Along with overtones of possible seduction.

She felt the tug of her own smile. One way to forget a storm. Or create their own if she wasn't careful.

The guy knew how to make the most of situations. She dug her nose out of his shirt and looked up at him but she had to lean back in his arms to gain some distance. 'No cheating.'

'Third time lucky?' Dark and dangerous eyes were brim full of wicked intent. 'I won't ask for anything you're unwilling to give,' he murmured as his head descended. 'But I will ask...'

The heat. That was her first thought as her traitorous mouth accepted and then returned his kiss with precocious enthusiasm. What was this recognition as if she'd been joined to this mouth many times? How could that be?

He bent again, less gently, and the kiss deepened, became more sensual than she'd imagined, more insidiously addictive than she'd bargained for.

Carmen merged into the burning pressure of his lips against hers, the drugging assault as their bodies melded, and the rising heat between that mocked the puny storm around them.

Then the coolness of his leaving as he skimmed her neck with hot lips leaving his own trail of electrical activity where before there'd been the chill of sleeting rain.

When he bent to brush his mouth between her breasts she had to hang on or she'd fall down.

Her fingers slid up to bury in hair like silk beneath her fingertips, as he tipped her backwards over his arm like the marauder he was and suddenly she felt like ripping open the buttons of her shirt to give him access.

Then he was back at her mouth and she was drowning.

A scatter of drips from the leaking roof splashed her hair and annoyingly penetrated the fog of arousal. Good grief. She'd kissed him back as wildly as he'd kissed her. Stop.

If she wasn't careful he'd take her on the picnic table behind them and she'd wrap her legs around him blithely with delight. She pushed her hand against his chest and eased at least her top half out of his embrace. They were a little exposed here.

'Whoa there, cowboy.'

He stopped, looked down at her, stared for a moment and then to her surprise he threw back his head and laughed. Really laughed and if she'd though him a handsome man before, this laughing God was a million light years ahead of any man she'd seen before.

He eased her away slowly, unpeeling her from where they were plastered together at the hip and with both hands he gently straightened her shirt.

'My apologies.' He raised his brows with amusement still vivid in his face. 'Cowgirl.' And that cracked her up.

They'd both grinned in the humour of the moment and they laughed together before he gathered himself and put her from him. Finally able to speak sensibly, he murmured, 'You are without doubt the most original woman. It is fortunate one of us has their wits about them.'

'You're pretty special yourself,' she muttered as she increased the distance another couple of centimetres – so she didn't reach out and touch him again.

Where had that sensual onslaught come from? And no little smooch. Good grief. She couldn't remember a kiss like that ever.

A year of marriage hadn't prepared her for that maelstrom. That mother of all kisses and she'd allowed his passion to overtake her. Met him with her own response enthusiastically. Still, it had been a wild half hour. She'd already been reeling with an adrenalin-laden birth and found herself plastered to a man in a picnic shelter during an electrical storm? Primal stuff. With such a man as Zafar.

She needed to get clear of this guy because already she was like one of those puddles the storm had just dumped. Wet, formless, muddied with lust. Soaked in it.

She glanced around and the inky front was noticeably lighter above them as it rolled out to sea. 'The storm seems to be passing. Let's get out of here while we can.'

He'd distanced from her too. She could feel it. Good. Maybe he regretted their detonation as well.

She watched as he removed the phone from his pocket, dialled, spoke in his own language, and then tucked it away. Had he done that to distance her too? 'Yusuf will pick us up from across the grass.'

'We can walk.'

But even as she finished speaking a long black car pulled up opposite the park. The henchman had been out there waiting in the storm anyway. Hopefully he hadn't been watching. Hadn't seen their embrace.

She shivered. So now she was cold without Zafar holding her? What the heck was she doing when she got close to this guy? Apparently whatever he wanted.

She needed to remember he was a man from a different world, a world where his bodyguard was always present, where a limousine appeared in moments and where she couldn't understand even his language – a man with his own rules. Rules that differed from hers no matter he'd lived and worked here once.

CHAPTER TEN - Zafar

Zafar pondered Carmen's silence and reassertion of her independence as he slid into the car after her. But he pondered his own response more.

What had happened?

The heat they'd created, the shock of unexpected connection, the loss of his own control had rocked him. Perhaps it was just his body requiring sex but he did not think so. Sex didn't mean loss of control. Either way it was not something to rush. This was a fundamnetal change he could sense in himself. Very unsettling.

He filed away the fire between this woman and his unknown self in the storm for future thought.

For the moment - he had decided he needed to secure her services for his cousin. Something he suspected would require careful negotiation.

He did not want her caring for other women. At the beck and call of others. He wanted her available for Fadia whenever she was needed. And possibly for him, a quiet voice inside suggested, but he pushed it away. He could imagine Carmen's response to that chauvinism. This was certainly a new direction for his usually introverted thoughts.

'I had hoped we would to discuss the possibility of you caring for Fadia as your only client.'

She shifted beside him and avoided his eyes in a swift turn to the outside world. 'There is no discussion.' Her words were clipped as if her mind was elsewhere and did not want to be disturbed. Almost in panic?

She was as unsettled as he was. Why did that amuse him? Because he was a man.

It seemed she could sense the strangeness of the shift between them too. 'That is not an answer. More a knee-jerk reaction I believe they call it.'

'I have a knee if you want one,' she muttered, and he wondered if he was supposed to hear that? Such a physical woman. More clearly she said, 'I'm afraid I can't help you.'

Why was she so sure of herself? She did not know him. Still, this woman could be most annoying. He restrained himself from correcting her. 'Because...?'

What was so absorbing outside the car that she must look past him out the window? 'Because I have two jobs already.'

Of course. She worked at the hospital. Fadia had said Carmen had been her midwife at the birth. No doubt these two jobs explained why she looked so tired. As to why... The money answer would be the simplest one. 'And why have you two jobs?'

'That's none of your business.'

He caught Yusuf's eye in the mirror and his driver nodded. Not yet but it soon would be. Perhaps Yusuf already had gleaned some information.

She went on, militantly, so obviously annoyed by his questions. 'If you wish Fadia to have a personal mothercraft nurse, of course you can arrange that but it won't be me.'

'I was thinking a professional midwife to act as flight assistant for Fadia on the trip to Zandorro and to help her settle in.'

'No. Thank you.' Such a prickly woman while still remaining polite. He suppressed a smile.

'A week or two only?' The look she gave him suggested he would get nowhere without a change of direction. He needed to find another way. 'Let's leave that for the moment. Tell me how this baby hotel works. Do all the midwives work at both the hospital labour wards and the hotel?'

She frowned as if collecting her thoughts. 'How did you know I worked at both places?'

'My cousin told me.' He liked that he had perplexed her. She narrowed her eyes at him but then looked away past him again. 'I do the occasional night shift at the hospital as well as the hotel, yes.'

Every time she did not tell the truth she looked away. A poor teller of lies. Then again that was not a bad thing. Fadia had said she worked three nights on the weekend, plus day shifts the five weekdays. That meant two double shifts a week. She had to be exhausted.

'We have eight beds on floors five and six in the hotel for the private patients who transfer from the hospital. Most new mothers stay two to four days before they go home.'

Ah. She'd answered his question about the baby hotel, a topic he'd moved on from in his head and it took a moment for him to refocus. He was interested in the concept. It could work in Zandorro. Perhaps even for the children's hospital. 'So, after the birth, when they wish, mothers transfer here?'

'That's correct. As Fadia did. If their birth was uncomplicated. And the midwives visit. The beauty of the hotel, as opposed to the hospital, is the mother's support people can stay. Friends can visit less rigidly than in a hospital.'

Like the man, Hassan, whom he wished to keep from his cousin. She looked away again.. Her complicity with Fadia was not something he wished to bring up now.

'Up to two other children may stay with the parents in their hotel rooms, and the access of the midwife means the transition period to home is less stressful than a busy ward in the hospital.'

'And the midwife provides what?'

'Help with feeding problems, settling techniques and to talk about postnatal needs out of the hospital environment. The hotel provides food and housekeeping.' She gestured to the world outside the car. 'The lovely part here is the view. Mums can gaze over the beach from their balcony. It's a great place to regather their resources before they go home.'

His attention caught. *Regather their resources.* He liked that concept. Just looking at this Carmen regathered his resources.

He hadn't realised how low his reserves had fallen until the elevator incident.

Yet the more he came into contact with this woman the more alive he felt. It seemed some time with the delectable Carmen could be as beneficial as the sojourn in the desert he'd prescribed himself.

If she was who she said she was.

When he knew more of her circumstances.

And he knew what Yusuf had turned up.

'That is all very interesting.' The car glided to a stop. 'We are back. Thank you for accompanying me and my apologies for your exposure to the weather.'

'I doubt even you have control over the weather.' She gave him a slightly mocking smile he did not appreciate and raised her hand to open her own door.

He was pleased to see her start of surprise when it opened from the outside. She would learn a woman should be cared for and protected. That he could care and protect her. If she would let him.

CHAPTER ELEVEN
– Carmen

Yusef opened her door before she could. The man must have dashed around to get here so fast. Carmen didn't like this henchman of Zafar's. Judging by the cold expression on Yusuf's face the feeling was mutual.

This man with a scar who did his master's bidding unsettled her.

Still, another two or three days and the lot of them would be gone, she thought as she climbed out of the car and slid past Yusef without touching him. She hoped Fadia found safety and peace with her decision. As her sons were heirs the decision had ramifications and risks.

She glanced back at the car but Zafar had exited and moved to her side. 'Oh. Goodnight.'

He took her hand, bowed over it briefly and then, slowly, deliberately turned her fingers to expose her wrist before he lifted it to his warm mouth. He kissed her skin.

The kiss lingered, featherlight but erotic, and her response from the intimate caress sent gooseflesh over her arms and chest.

Still not fully recovered from the passion in the storm that small touch shock waves surging back through her that weakened her knees. She hoped that explained the absolute melting of every bone in her body as he lifted his lips from her skin. Good grief.

She turned away shakily, ignored the expressionless face of Yusuf, and passed through the doors into the lobby to use the lift to the car park. She doubted her suddenly wobbly legs would be able to traverse the steep driveway down to her car without falling over.

Her wrist felt branded and she rode down the lift pressing her fingers to the spot as if to contain the imprint. Get a grip, she warned herself fiercely. He's just a man. You're out of practice and your hormones pulled the magic Zafar carpet out from under you.

Driving home blurred, automatic pilot obedient, as her brain whirled and her eyes strayed to her wrist near the steering wheel.

What was she doing? What was he doing? Did he have intentions of seduction?

Why? Did he want his cousin watched so badly he thought she might be useful? And was she tempted?

When she arrived at the door of her block of flats a group of youths called out and waved towards her. A bottle smashed into the gutter across the road and not surprisingly she fumbled with the lock and she dropped her keys in the dark. She scooped them up quickly and searched again for the correct key. Her heart speeding and neck prickling in her haste to get safely inside.

Someone called out, approached the youths, and spoke to them harshly. Whatever was said worked because they turned and hurried back the other way. Her neck felt exposed and she resisted the urge to peer into the gloom at her Good Samaritan across the road. Which was ridiculous, wasn't it?

Once the4 door was open she glanced uneasily over her shoulder but she couldn't see anyone. She slipped inside and shut the door. Bolted it.

Her eyes scratched with tiredness and she just hope that blasted Zafar hadn't interfered with her ability to sleep. Managing the next four days depended on this good night's sleep before she started work at lunchtime tomorrow and Thursday, then after work Friday, night duty would begin again.

She felt the frustration gather as she contemplated the unrelenting schedule.

As Tilly said, working seven days a week was crazy but it was only for another six months until she'd paid all the debts her husband had left her with. She wanted her credit rating back.

When she'd been offered the Baby Hotel job, which paid well, finally she had her head above water. If she needed to work seven days a week for another few months, at least she loved both jobs.

Carmen stripped off her clothes, hurriedly showered and fell into bed.

Lord she was tired.

Carmen slept deeply despite being seduced by her dreams – wonderful, stretch-like-a-cat-and-purr dreams – and the wisps of memories remained when the sun rose and left her with a small kink in her lips that peeped out while she brushed her teeth.

'You need a swim,' she admonished the sultry-eyed woman in the mirror. 'In fact you need a freezing cold shower.' But still she smiled. Her skin belonged to a womanly her and not the machine-like work person she'd turned into even if her "admirer" was some nebulous dream man with a magical mouth.

She rubbed her arms. Scrummy dreams that left her feeling warm. She wished she could bottle them and pull this feeling out when she needed it.

Life seemed a lot more interesting than it had two days ago and she couldn't pretend it had nothing to do with a certain dark-eyed prince.

She glanced out the window of her cramped room and the sun shone onto the road enticing her to play. She hadn't done much of that for a while either – more work and worry than play.

The morning stretched ahead before her shift at one pm and she decided to pack a small lunch and head to the beach.

Coogee glittered with tourists. Sun-loving mums toted babies to play in the waves and reminded her why she'd preferred to live in a bedsit here than a roomy unit somewhere else.

Carmen dropped her towel and bag on the white sand and shed her sarong along with the cares of the last weeks. Suddenly life was too short and the waves beckoned with their walls of cheeky fish daring her to join them. The fish scattered into the white wash as she splashed through the tingling freshness of the surf with a grin on her face.

CHAPTER TWELVE
–Zafar

Zafar watched her run in his direction. She hadn't seen him because her smile shone like the sun, more carefree than he had ever seen, oblivious, and outshone even the brightness of the sparkling bay.

Inside, he felt the shift. His gut clenched and his body stirred. This visceral response was not from the emotions of an unexpected birth or a wild storm. His body quickened with the promise of her bare skin close to his. There was no doubt this woman drew him like mythical mermaids drew sailors to rocks, attraction destined for disaster if he wasn't careful, but still he pushed through the wash towards her.

It seemed the cost to feel alive required some threat to his peace of mind.

She surfaced and wiped the water from her face, squeezing and shaking her hair like a boisterous puppy, but it was the jiggle of her body that deepened his voice as he hailed her. 'I had forgotten the delights of an Australian beach.'

He watched her expression change from carefree to careful and the sight saddened him, he didn't know why, becasue in the last two years he would never have noticed such a thing.

She recovered quickly. 'Prince Zafar?' He was beginning to think this woman would recoup in any circumstances.

'Please, Zafar. We are not in a formal situation.'

He saw the crinkle of amusement in her eyes as she glanced around at the water and the frolicking children. 'No. Not formal at all.' She may even be laughing at him and he didn't mind if she was. It was worth it to see her expression relax once more, the smile back in her eyes. How perplexing for his state of mind.

'Is this what you do before work?'

She looked around again. 'Not enough, but I'm going to make concerted effort to do it more often.' She looked away from him and spread her arms. 'Isn't it glorious.'

His blood heated. 'The view is indeed spectacular.' He needed to direct his energies elsewhere or he would pull that delicious body against him and who knew where that would lead. 'Do you swim well?'

'Better than you,' she tossed over her shoulder as she dived into the next wave and struck out for the centre of the bay.

A challenge. Enticing. And irresistible.

We will see, he thought with satisfaction as he followed her with a powerful overarm stroke that soon had them level out past the breakers. They stopped and floated. 'You were saying?'

She grinned across at him and a wave slapped her in the cheek so she choked and coughed. He laughed back at her and she trod water until she had her breath again.

She tossed her head. 'You might have speed but I could swim all day.'

He raised his brows and his voice lowered. 'In my youth... I was famous for my stamina.'

To his delight she blushed. A delectable warning of danger for both of them. 'A race to the beach then.'

She didn't answer. Just turned and swam and this time he outpaced her so that when she arrived, breathless, he was waiting for her. She swam well. As well as any woman he'd seen but she'd pushed herself hard to catch him. A hint of competitiveness he admired. He couldn't help teasing her.

'Such deep breathing.' And a delightful sight he enjoyed as her breasts rose and fell. 'Perhaps you would like me to carry you up to your towel?'

She stood up and rested her hands on her knees to catch her breath. 'Never. I would rather crawl there myself.'

'I believe you.' He inclined his head. The words came unexpected. 'Perhaps we could share lunch before your work.'

She shook her head. 'Not a good idea to have lunch with one of my patient's relatives.'

Who would presume to judge? 'I see nothing wrong with it.'

She tilted her head at him as if he were an interesting specimen she'd found on the beach. 'Of course you don't.'

'The opinions of others are the least of my worries. You are afraid to spend time with me?'

She narrowed her eyes at him and he withheld his satisfied smile. She didn't like that. Baiting this woman warmed his cold soul when it shouldn't.

She huffed out a sigh. 'Only if I pay my share.' Capitulation, though not complete, was sweet. It was a long time since he'd tasted sweet.

But he did not charge women for food. He shrugged. 'Not possible.'

'Then you eat on your own.' She began to wade through the water towards the beach, not looking to see if he followed but as he watched the swing of her hips he wondered if she knew she drew him like magnet. It was indeed an unexpectedly glorious day.

'Perhaps you would wish to pay for my meal.'

She stopped and looked back at him and a small throaty chuckle delighted him. 'You're on.'

Fanciful, fanciful, thought.

CHAPTER THIRTEEN – Carmen

Later, at the Baby Hotel during midwife handover, Carmen heard that Fadia and her babies were managing splendidly. Her smile spread. Clever, clever Fadia. Funny how much she was looking forward to seeing her and the young princes.

They went on to discuss the other mothers and their plans for discharge. As she took over their care Carmen left Fadia to last, because no doubt that would be the longest visit. That way the other families would know where she was if they needed her urgently. One mention of twins and the mums were instantly sympathetic.

Strangely, Yusuf was not at his usual post and outside Fadia's door, so that as she knocked and waited a moment for Fadia's call to come in, she glanced around before she used her key. A tall swarthy man approached her and Carmen instantly recognised him from the photograph.

'Excuse me? You are the midwife?' He smiled, flashy white teeth in an insincere smile as he eyed her up and down. Nope. She didn't feel flattered. Or reassured that Hassan was a nice man.

'Yes?' She withdrew her hand from the door lock.

'I wish to visit my friend, Fadia Smith. Can you tell me which room she is in?'

'I could.' She smiled at him. 'But then I'd have to kill you.'

As soon as the words left her mouth she regretted them. His face darkened and he looked even more like her ex. Perhaps the wrong ethnic background to get her Australian humour but the words had slipped out possibly because she'd felt suddenly nervous. Not the time for levity.

Before anything else could be said, Zafar appeared from the fire escape. The man took one look at him and turned to disappear down the corridor in the direction of the lifts.

Fadia's voice floated through the door. 'Come in. Is that you, Carmen?' She looked at Zafar and his frown and decided discretion was the better part of valour.

She swiped the card and opened the door. 'Yes.' She stepped inside and held the door for Zafar as if nothing had happened.

His eyes held hers. 'Did he threaten you?'

'No. But he might have. I think your timing excellent.'

'I hope it continues to be so.'

He opened his mouth to say more but she shook her head as she mouthed 'later.' He followed her into the room and nodded at his cousin. 'You look rested.'

'Thank you.' Fadia smiled at them both and looked much happier. 'They've been perfect. Asleep most of the morning.'

'I will return shortly.' Zafar nodded and swept out again and Fadia raised her brows.

'Zafar was coming down the corridor just as you called for me to come in. Maybe he thought I was going to throw him out again.' They hid smiles behind their hands. 'But tell me, they've both been sleeping?'

'Since six o'clock. I managed by myself. I can't believe it.'

'They'll wake up soon. Most likely for the next twenty-four hours they'll feed more often. Be prepared. Then it will settle down. You're doing amazingly well.' She was talking to Fadia but her thoughts were divided. Judging by the expression on Zafar's face he'd taken off after Fadia's thwarted visitor.

Seeing the man had been unsettling but useless speculation on what was happening wouldn't help anyone.

Carmen went through the bath routine and by the time they'd finished she'd been there over an hour.

'I'll be off to see the other ladies. Just give me a ring if you need me. You could realx and enjoy the view over the beach.'

Fadia nodded. 'It's hard to imagine that one day my boys will be big enough to run on the sand. I would like to sit and picture that day.'

The whole shift passed without Zafar since that brief sighting in the corridor, which she would have liked to discuss, but the opportunity didn't arrive. Yusuf stood by the limosine as she drove out of the car park on her way home. What went on in the henchman's head, she wondered, and then decided she didn't want to know.

Whatever it was his master had ordered it.

The next day she started early and as Carmen approached Fadia's room the sound of distressed babies and their mother's sobs soaked through the door.

She used the keycard that hung around her neck to slip in. The noise dumped on her like a wall of sand from a collapsed sandcastle and hastily she shut the door.

'Fadia? Honey? Are you okay?' She could see that she wasn't.

The girl lay face down on the bed shuddering into the mattress, the twins bellowed in their cots, red-faced and in unison as they waved their tight little fists. Locked in with them all, for a moment Carmen felt every minute of lost sleep from the last two months. Then her brain kicked into gear.

Babies first to lower the noise level seemed a good place to start. She unwrapped Harrison, always the loudest, deftly changed his sodden nappy which slowed the high-pitched roar to a hiccough, and re-wrapped him in a new bunny rug before placing him back in his bed.

Then she did the same for Braxton and popped him in with his brother so the two, tiny, wrapped bundles lay facing each other, faces creased with little frowns. The quiet wouldn't last long.

'Fadia. What's happened?' The girl sobbed more dramatically into her sodden pillow and Carmen glanced around. 'What's going on? Sit up, honey.'

Slowly she rose and showed her tearstained face. 'Tom sent a note this morning to say goodbye.' She sniffed. 'The boys have fed every two hours since midnight. I had little sleep and I'm so tired. I choose Zandorro anyway, but Hassan was my last link to my husband. It makes me so sad for what I have lost.'

Carmen wondered if Zafar had anything to do with Hassan's blessed absence but for the moment the unsettled children were most pressing. 'Of course, I understand.'

Fadia wasn't listening. 'It will be good when I get to Zandorro. I'm not managing as well as I thought I would.'

'You're being hard on yourself.' Poor Fadia. Day three after two babies. Baby blues as well most likely. 'Yesterday was too good and it's payback today.' She sat on the bed next to her. Softly she said, 'You've had a very tragic start to your family. On top of all that you have two babies that need you every minute. I think you've been amazing.'

Fadia sniffed tragically. 'But yesterday everything was going so well.'

'And today is a difficult day for you. Three days after birth is a notorious time for feeling sad and overwhelmed.'

She waved at the boys who were grumbling ominously. 'With twins, two are hungry and feeding more often to bring your milk in. There's twice as many hormones floating around and with so little sleep of course you're going to be fragile.'

Fadia sniffed. 'I thought I could manage.'

'And you are. Amazingly. But perhaps help from family is a good answer for now.'

She glanced at the window. 'I'm sure the last thing Hassan wants is for you to lose sleep over him.' She wasn't really.

If Hassan was as much like her ex as he looked, she doubted he thought of anyone but himself.

There was a knock on the door and Carmen's heart sank. Visitors were the last thing Fadia needed now, but Fadia nodded for her to let them in. When she opened the door she already suspected it would be Zafar.

He narrowed his eyes at his cousin's red face and puffy eyes. 'Yusuf says there is a problem?'

'Good old Yusuf,' Carmen muttered under her breath.

As if to support his comment both babies began to cry again and Carmen sighed. She wasn't even going to go near the Hassan fiasco.

'Babies need feeding, mothers need sleep. It's a day for feeling blue.' She looked at Fadia who teetered on the verge of casting herself into her pillow again. 'Fadia, perhaps you could wash your face while we mind your sons?'

Reluctantly, the girl heaved herself off her bed and Carmen picked up Harrison and handed him to Zafar. 'Here. See how you are with princes. One each.' She scooped up Braxton and tucked him into her shoulder and patted the nappied bottom.

She shouldn't have been surprised when Zafar did the same, calmly and confidently, and even cross little Harry seemed to understand the command to settle. He even twitched his mouth in a windy smile at his uncle.

The picture made her chest feel tight. 'You're very good at that.'

His brows rose. 'Should I not be?'

Made sense. The man had to love kids if he studied paediatrics. She had the feeling this man could do anything. And do it well. 'I'd forgotten you specialised in children. Your talents are wasted.'

CHAPTER FOURTEEN – Zafar

'I will practice again, one day.' As soon as my duties allow. He stroked Braxton's bunny-wrapped back in slow steady waves and stared down at the baby's soft dark hair. So like Samir's. 'I had personal experience with children. My infant son.'

He could feel her gaze, intent, arrested, but he didn't look up. He did not want her sympathy. Only for her to understand that he was damaged. Instead, he stroked the warm spine of his nephew and spoke to the downy head. 'My wife and small son died in the same hijacking that almost killed me.'

He glanced out the window and added flatly, 'Of course I wish I too had died. You can imagine my horror when I woke as a survivor.'

Zafar felt the tightness of grief again in his chest. Why on earth was he telling her? His hands tightened as he looked down at his nephew. 'I remember the weight of my son in my arms. The way he smiled.' Being here with these children reminded him so forcibly.

'That's terrible. I'm sorry.' She waved her hand helplessly. 'That's bland but I don't intent it to be. I wish I had better words. Your family has had so much tragedy.'

Yes, they had. He looked her way, but he wasn't seeing her. Keeping his voice devoid of anything she could offer sympathy to. 'It was two years ago but I remember how to care for a baby.'

Fadia returned from the bathroom and Zafar ended the conversation as he spoke to her. 'You are exhausted. Now will you have a mothercraft nurse?'

Fadia looked at him, turned and ran sobbing back into the bathroom and shut the door. He closed his eyes. That had been abrupt from the emotions he was still fighting back. Now he's upset his cousin.

Carmen didn't say a word. But her ire simmered around her like a cloak. She patted her charge's back once more and placed him back in his cot before she turned to Fadia's bed and straightened it. As if she needed to do something with her hands or she'd strangle him.

He may have deserved that. 'Nothing to say?'

She glared at him. He could almost hear her thoughts. *So much she could say.* 'Nothing you don't already know.' Yet her voice came out calmly. 'You may have skills with babies but you're not that hot with new mums.'

He flinched. Calm but with bite. And deserved. How to explain when he was unversed in explaining himself to anyone. Why for her? For Carmen. 'I struggle with her wish to be without help when she has had such difficulties.'

Like the woman in front of him. Of the incident Yusef had told him. This woman against the world alone. 'Of your desire also to do this. I wish to speak of something else...'

'Forgive me, but I have been told your husband proved a poor choice? This is correct?' He knew he looked anything but apologetic.

'How do you know of my marriage? My background? My story?

'I have made enquiries.'

At his words her face paled. 'I don't want to think about how you found out. How much you think you know. Stop poking into my affairs? she said sharply.

His gaze fixed on her. His own disgust for the man who did this to her in his voice. 'He swindled you out of your home and left you with debts.'

'Who told you that?'

He ignored her question. 'You live in a troubled area. Live alone unprotected? Yusuf spoke to men who accosted you.'

Carmen shook her head in disbelief and he could not miss the absolute beacon of anger that flared at his intrusion into her private life.

Perhaps he should not have shared that. But he wanted honesty between them not lies or subterfuge. Nor would he have it undone.

CHAPTER FIFTEEN
—Carmen

Bile simmered up from her stomach and into her throat. The men in the alley. The smashed bottle. She did remember that incident. Yusef had been the one who chased them away. But it didn't matter. She would have managed. How dare he have her spied on.

What mattered was he'd had her followed. Like her ex had done that after she left him. This intrusion of privacy made her feel more vulnerable than any random gang of youths.

'You're as bad as him. How dare you? Neither of you have the right to stalk me.'

Another horror of a man who didn't think like a normal person. The wet washer of reality. He was of a royal and privileged line and never would be normal. And she'd been attracted to him.

She wasn't sure who she was more angry with, him or herself, for being drawn to him.

He shrugged. 'Privacy can be bought.'

'Not my privacy, buster.' And to think she'd kissed him with abandon in a storm.

His head went up. The arrogant prince very much in evidence and she reminded herself he was just as high-handed about Fadia. No wonder the girl had misgivings about returning with him. No wonder she wanted Carmen to come and stand up for her.

She lifted her head and glared. 'What an attractive person you are.'

His eyes narrowed. 'Sarcasm does not become you, Carmen.'

'Funny.' She couldn't remember ever being this angry. Not even with Carl. She sucked air in trying to calm herself so that her words came out low and biting. 'Yet bullying suits you very well.'

He brushed that off. 'I am not ashamed of my actions.'

She almost laughed in his face. 'Why am I not surprised?'

'You would be wise to hold your tongue.'

So, she'd pushed him too far. Carmen stamped down the cowardly urge to do what she was told. Tough biscuits. 'Hold your own. I've met men like you before. I married an arrogant, self-important bully and I won't be bullied or tricked,' she paused, hissed the words out, 'or followed... again. Ever!'

Despite her low tone anger vibrated in her voice and she wasn't sure she could contain it. The child in her arms shifted and whimpered and she blew out a breath. She still wasn't sure if she was more wild with him or herself. The air quivered with tension before she spun around and walked to the door.

'You are not leaving. You cannot walk out in the middle of this discussion.'

'Discussion?' She snorted her derision. 'I can and will do as I wish. I'm no woman in your harem. I'm not under you employ.'

She called through the bathroom door, 'I'll be back in a few minutes, Fadia,' and let herself out before he could stop her.

As she walked down the corridor to her room anger bubbled and popped like a little lava pool from sudden volcanic eruption. She didn't do loss of control. Someone had to remain rational. She rarely did anger because she prided herself on her control.

That was how she escaped her marriage. Level head. Planning. What was it about this man that pushed all the buttons of high emotion?

Her eyes narrowed as she concentrated on any sound of his pursuit. Listened for the sound of the door opening but heard nothing. She could feel Yusuf's frown follow her as she increased the distance between them, could admit she was ridiculously glad his chair was near the lifts and not positioned at her end of her corridor.

She should have shut the door to the midwife's room but she refused to have them think she was scared. She really did like the mums to feel they could poke their heads in any time.

Yet couldn't help the jump in her pulse rate when Yusuf appeared.

The burly guard folded his muscular arms. 'Prince Zafar wishes to see you in his suite.'

She didn't stand, looked over her shoulder at him from her chair. 'Tell him I'm busy.' And now she could go back to Fadia if he was gone.

His eyes narrowed and he took a step towards her. 'You will come now.'

And you are dreaming, Carmen mentally snarled. She stood up and casually reached for her handbag and rummaged around inside.

'Should I comb my hair?' She removed the small can of attacker spray a friend had given her when she'd first divorced Carl.

Straightened and lifted her chin. Waved the can at him. 'Do you know what this is? Paint. It won't hurt you but they say it takes a week to wash off.' Her voice remained pleasant. 'Now, please tell Prince Zafar that I'm busy.'

Just before she left for Fadia's room her phone rang. Zafar sounded amused. She doubted Yusuf was. 'So, I must come to you?'

'Or not. I really am busy.'

'I apologise for interrupting your valuable work. I did not intend to bully you.'

An apology? She hadn't expected that. It set her back for a second before she lifted her chin. 'You tried. But I left.' She may have over-reacted but the pain was still raw from her shattered illusions in the past and perhaps a few from the present. 'I'm touchy on the subject of stalkers.'

Still, an apology was something her ex had never mastered.

Zafar spoke again. 'I wish to apologise personally. I also want to discuss Fadia with you. Perhaps we could find a time that you are not busy. Or at work.'

There were no times like that.

His voice. 'Dinner? If I were to arrange a table in my suite for seven thirty? That would be half an hour after you finish your shift tonight.'

Didn't he realise he was being arrogant and pushy again? Perhaps it was a failing with royalty as well as ex-husbands. Shame he couldn't see her sarcastic salute.

He went on. 'That would give you time to change.'

Unbelievable. Like she had a cocktail dress in her handbag? 'Change? From my uniform into my sarong and swimmers you mean?'

There was silence. 'Whatever you choose to wear will be acceptable.'

'Gee, thanks, but no thanks.'

He sighed. 'You are tiresome with your objections.'

'Heaven forbid.' She swallowed the hysterical laugh that wanted to escape. She needed to shut the lid on the box of memories he'd opened and a cosy dinner wouldn't help.

There was silence on the end of the phone.

It went on until she was the one who felt like a petulant child. Not fair. To her own disgust she thought of poor Fadia, how much she needed her support, relented. 'Oh, very well. I'll see what I can find.'

She put the phone down gently but her heart pounded in a way that wasn't gentle at all.

She should not have agreed.

But she had.

Not smart.

She could just picture herself sitting in the suite in her uniform, or her sarong, and she couldn't deny the fact that she didn't like the picture.

The last thing she needed to feel was at a disadvantage dressed like an employee or a beach bum. And she had no time.

She picked up the phone again and spoke to the best Concierge in Sydney, Donna, her friend from downstairs, always good value and resourceful.

'A cheap dress that looks good? There's a great specials bin in the boutique. I know what you need. I'll send something up in your size, no worries. Do it all the time for guests.'

The hands of the wall clock seemed to turn twice as fast as the afternoon sped by in a blur of breastfeeding issues, baby weights and newborn bathing demonstrations.

The second time she visited Fadia, the girl seemed to have recovered her composure and Carmen wondered if now that Hassan was not a problem Fadia would come into her own. Carmen had no doubt that Fadia had a strength that would astound her cousin.

Perhaps Hassan had played to Fadia's emotions to keep the girl dependant.

Her mind twisted and turned as she prepared to take blood from the twins for their newborn screening tests. Fadia grimaced as the lancet pierced Braxton's heel. She breastfed them one at a time to help distract them from the sting of the lancet prick.

When it was over, and they'd tucked the boys back into their little beds, Fadia shook her head in disbelief. 'But they didn't cry?'

'Because you fed them at the same time.'

'I'm glad it helped.' Then another worried frown creased her brows. 'If I go to Zandorro and the results come back with a problem, how will they find me?'

Ahh, she'd decided.

It would be hard here with her babies on her own and she couldn't help her instinct that Zafar was a much safer bet than a man like Hassan. 'The results go to your doctor. We would find you and follow up.'

Fadia put her hand out. 'Are you sure there's no chance you could come with me? Just for a little while?' Her dark eyes pleaded. 'You help without fuss and make me feel more confident. I would not be as nervous if you were with me.'

Had Zafar told her to ask? 'I'm sorry, Fadia. I can't. I have my job here. But you will be strong.' Carmen gestured to the sleeping babies. 'For your boys. You are their world. Nobody can ever change that.'

'I'm afraid that once I'm back, the older women will try to take over.'

She hugged Fadia. 'Maybe a mothercraft nurse from here isn't such a bad idea. Someone whose loyalties lie with you? I'm sure Zafar would agree.'

She shook her head. 'I want you. Just for a few weeks?'

Such imploring eyes and Carmen could feel herself weaken. Then she thought of Zafar. Of her response to him. Of being under his 'rule.' A disturbing thought.

But then, it was also disturbing to think of Fadia being without a champion.

'I don't think I can. It's a long way to go for something a lot of people could do. I'll think about it but it's unlikely, I'm sorry. I'll see you in the morning. Make sure you ask the night midwife if you need help.'

By the time she'd written up her notes and handed over to her colleague it was seven fifteen.

Carmen used the midwife's bathroom to wash and pulled the new dress from the bag to check out the tag. Slashed price, non-iron and machine washable. She loved Donna.

Carmen shivered with the silky slide of fabric down her body and she hoped it wasn't an omen. Maybe she should wear her uniform. What was she doing anyway trying to impress a Prince with her bargain bin clothes?

She shook her head at herself.

No. She was dressing for herself and it looked good. Felt good. Gave her power.

Even if the maroon fabric did plunge a little into her cleavage but that was fixed with the cream silk scarf Donna had added. The pair of slip-on half heels were perfect as was the costume jewellery. God bless her favourite concierge.

At least she wouldn't feel like the poor relation in Zafar's luxury suite.

Mascara and lipstick would do if she didn't want to be late... Carmen paused with lipstick in hand in front of the mirror. Did she want to be late?

She smiled at herself. She'd probably pulled enough tails today. In fact, she'd take her attacker dye.

'Evening, Yusuf.' The man's eyes glittered at her as he stood up to accompany her. 'I can find my own way.'

He bowed impassively. 'Yet I will accompany you.'

He didn't have to ask her to wait while he opened the heavy door at the top of the stair well. She guessed she'd learned some of the rules at least. It was funny how they all opted for the stairs now.

While she waited, she remembered the first time she'd stood here like this. Was it only three days ago? So much had happened.

So much that her world might prove a little flat when all these unusual people moved on from her life.

In the hallway the other guard, still standing like before, watched them approach. She doubted he even leant against the wall when he was tired.

Yusuf knocked and the same woman opened it. *Déjà vu*.

As she walked past her, the woman inclined her head in deference. Carmen frowned. She was pretty sure she didn't do that last time.

She still pondered that gesture when Zafar's door opened and he came through, dressed in tailored slacks and a silk shirt – a very poor attempt at not looking like a million dollars.

'*As asaalum al aikum*. Peace be with you.' He smiled.

Nice of him to translate for her. 'Good evening.'

'Now, why did I think you would be late?'

Carmen shrugged. 'Because you don't know me?'

'But I will,' was said quietly, and she frowned.

He gestured to the cushions spread on the carpet beside a low table and then a table and chairs on the veranda.

Conversationally, he said, 'Would you prefer to sit inside or out? Fatima will lay the table.'

She glanced out the door to the balcony, screened from other guests by a metal lattice and with northern view over Coogee it would be criminal to waste. Lots of air space around them if not physical distance.

And she'd rather be at eyelevel with him on a chair. 'Outside, please.'

He nodded to Fatima who picked up a wicker basket and moved to the veranda where she proceeded to produce everything needed like Mary Poppins – or more appropriately a robed genie – out of the bag. When the table had been set, she disappeared into the tiny kitchen and wheeled out a trolley with dishes of food.

Zafar picked up a bottle from a stand of ice. 'Perhaps I could pour you a drink while we wait. Champagne?'

Something to settle the seagulls from outside that had landed in her stomach perhaps. It seemed this was not against his religion, then? The way she felt at the moment... 'Champagne would be lovely.'

He held the glass and she reached for it carefully, ridiculously anxious not to touch his fingers, until his eyes met hers.

He knew. And with that one glance he knew she knew.

She frowned, decided not to play the game and took it firmly. His fingers tingled against her own.

'Thank you.'

He turned away but not before she could see his amusement.

Carmen looked towards Fatima and took a couple of calming breaths. The servant had arranged dishes of food and napkins beside a huge flat dish of white rice. Perhaps sliced lamb roast? She recognised the bowls of stuffed tomatoes, a dark and aromatic stew with lime green beans wafted amazing aroma her way, along with several dishes she didn't recognise. Surely far too much for just the two of them.

'Ah. Fatima is finished.' He tilted his head at his servant. 'Leave.' The woman bowed and left the room.

She slowed, turned to look at him, and said distinctly as she moved out to the balcony, 'Now, I find that, offensive.'

'Why? Because I asked my servant to depart.'

Carmen lifted her chin. 'Please is free.' His eyes were crinkled with amusement. It seemed she was hilarious, Carmen considered her options.

She must have looked dangerous because he held out his hands in apology. 'I couldn't resist. I imagine you with Mace pointed at Yusuf.'

She narrowed her eyes at him. 'Mace is illegal. It was coloured dye for self-defence.'

He laughed. And looked ten years younger for it. This handsome, ridiculously wealthy man so accustomed to his servants obeying his every command, laughed at her rebuke. He'd be accustomed to women falling at his feet not biting back.

Still he watched her. Still with amusement in his eyes. 'Did you bring it?'

Now what was he talking about. 'I'm sorry?'

'Your pressure pack protection.'

She smiled. 'You'll never know.'

For a moment she thought he was going to ask to see her purse. He didn't and it felt as though she'd won a small victory. It made her wonder why he didn't become more impatient with her lack of amenability. Why it seemed to amuse him so easily. 'How can you be so normal at times and so arrogant at others?'

'With you?' He'd read her mind again. 'I'm still working that out. It is novel for me. I was born into privilege, which I assure you comes with responsibility, but I studied in England and latterly Australia. You have very good schools – if a school system that levels a young man so he understands your abhorrence of our feudal system, is a good school.'

Carmen couldn't help smiling at that. She could imagine.

'I understand a little of the differences between you and the women in my culture.' He pulled out her chair and waited for her to sit. 'But I am, first of all, a prince of my country and second the travelled man. I am not without power. Perhaps it would be wise for you to remember that.'

He sat opposite and she took a sip of her drink to fill the silence between them. When she put her drink down she did have something to say. 'I'm angry you had me investigated.'

'I noticed.'

Well at least she'd got that point across.

He went on. 'It is as well we discuss this now.'

He leaned across to top up her glass but she covered it with her hand. 'I need my wits with you.'

He put the bottle back and she noticed he wasn't drinking. 'I'm flattered.' He didn't look it.

'Don't be.'

She thought he was going to follow up on her comment but in the end he changed tack. Hitched the sleeve of his right hand and gestured to the food. 'Eat. Please.'

Carmen carefully transferred some rice and a tomato to her plate with her knife and fork. She couldn't bring herself to use her fingers. There was something erotically earthy about a man eating slowly with his fingers.

'Try this,' he said. He picked up a sliver of something which turned out to be aromatic lamb, which she obediently tasted but the taste was nothing to the feel of his fingers against her mouth and her stomach kicked at that sensation.

'Please don't feed me.'

CHAPTER SIXTEEN – Zafar

Zafar wanted to do more than that. He could not take his eyes off her. He savoured the play of light across her skin as her expression changed like the ocean in front of them. Her sense of humour amused him – she made him smile more than he'd smiled for a long time – and her anger was so transparent because she made no attempt to disguise when he annoyed her.

A new experience for a woman to show her displeasure and probably good for his soul. No doubt a concept that would have amused his departed mother. And angered his father.

This fork in his thought process had continued since the woman's birth in the park. Since the way Carmen had cared for her. He wasn't sure why it had made such an impact except perhaps the focus and calmness of the woman opposite. No drama. No thought for herself. No expectation of anything except the perfect outcome. When he'd been practising his profession he'd often dealt with newborns at birth but drama had always been a part of that.

'I rang the hospital today to see how our mother and baby were doing.'

Had she read his mind? If so, she would have read more than she bargained for. He bit back a smile. 'And are they well?'

She smiled at him, her face lighting with delight, and he took the gift of that and stored it away in a corner of his cold heart.

'You know they are. You checked as well. I understand they haven't seen a flower arrangement so exotically expensive for years. Jenny feels very special.'

He had pleased her. 'I am glad. I am not always the arrogant bully you called me.' And that the mother also was happy, though not as important as Carmen's unexpected pleasure, was also good. He watched her expression as she tasted the rice and she cocked her head as if savouring it. Not a subtle tang she would be used to.

He went on. 'In Fadia's room I upset you.' When she would have spoken he held up his hand. He needed to say this but he was not skilled in apology. 'I beg your forgiveness for that. Holding Fadia's child brought back the reality of my loss. A factor in why I behaved badly towards you.'

She looked less than convinced but inclined her head. 'I accept your apology. Perhaps there is more to you when you're not having people investigated.'

'Tsk. So hard on me.'

She shrugged, unrepentant, and he imagined how it would feel to pull her into his arms and seduce her bravado away. The time was not right for weakness like that, could never be, while his role lay in the royal household. It was too dangerous for her.

Where were his barriers? His safeguards to creating an attachment? His loyalty to the memory of his wife.

He lifted his chin. 'My investigation of you was carried out because I wish to offer you a short tenure as Fadia's assistant. Given the status of her sons, it is not so much a matter of my arrogance as a matter of our national security. I trust that you accept this, not as an excuse, but as a reason.'

CHAPTER SEVENTEEN – Carmen

Something else was going on in his mind that was outside the conversation. Carmen could sense, almost feel it. The formality of his words was also a slight withdrawal. As if he felt he'd told her too much.

She opened her mouth to refute any reason was good enough for prying but he held up his hand. To her utter disgust she waited obediently again.

'I needed to be sure Fadia and her sons would be safe with you.'

She pointed to her mouth. 'So, I can talk now?'

He nodded good-naturedly and she realised she was in danger of sounding ill-tempered. How did he put her in the wrong when he was the chauvinist?

Carmen straightened the scarf around her shoulders as if to gather her control closer to her chest then counted to three. She spoke in her professionally calm voice. 'I see Fadia's need, but I am a midwife, not a mothercraft nurse. I'm afraid you've wasted your money on this investigation.'

'I disagree. You are excellent at your profession. Fadia likes you and needs a friend.' He shrugged. 'So that is enough for me. I wish to secure your services.'

'It seems she lost a friend today.' She tilted her head at him.

'Did she?'

'I gather Hassan is not in the picture anymore?'

Zafar questioned her blandly. 'Is he not?'

She decided he looked lazily ruthless. And disgustingly attractive with it. So now she was attracted to dangerous men? What was happening to her? 'I'm asking you. He is conspicuous by his non-appearance since that one time I spoke to him outside Fadia's door.'

'Do you assume I have done something to cause his absence?' No answer to her question, just one of his own.

'Don't look so surprised.' As if. He didn't look surprised at all.

'It is my intention to be aware of things that are my concern.' He added some lamb to her plate.

Now they were down to the meat of the matter. 'Then be concerned for your niece's state of mind. With Hassan off the scene she will be alone again and she has already lost her husband. Safeguards need to be in place. She's afraid she will lose control of her boys to those already living in your palace. To older relatives in power and wishes to be sure she won't suffer reduced access to her sons.'

She saw the understanding. 'Ah.' He leaned forward and pinned her with his full attention. 'I thank you for sharing that.' He shook his head obviously pained. 'I would not have that happen. I have learned the difficult choice my mother had to make. Having lost my own son, I know that feeling of emptiness and cost.'

His sincerity made her throat tighten. She put down her cutlery, unable to deal with food as her throat closed.

He pinned her with his gaze. 'Believe me. I will champion Fadia and wish only the best for her in this difficult time. Hence the need for you to consider my request that you accompany her for at least a short time.'

And Fadia had pleaded as well.

Could she? Carmen pushed temptation behind her and looked away. There were too many variables for that course. Too many dangers and one of the most dangerous sat opposite. 'I've already told you I have two jobs.'

He brushed that aside. 'And almost too tired to do either. You work at least seventy hours a week on mixed shifts. Why? For money. Ridiculous.'

See, she admonished herself. *He'd been checking up again.* 'That's none of your business.'

He ignored that. Perhaps he ignored everything people said that he didn't agree with. 'I believe you have holiday leave owing?'

Yes, but none she could take without a big drop in pay. How was she discussing this? 'I suppose you have that in writing from my employers?'

'I have verbal confirmation which is sufficient.' He shrugged that inconvenience away. 'What if I offered to clear all your debts for the sake of two weeks work in Zandorro with Fadia?'

She'd forgotten he knew about the debts. It was obscene to have that much money to tempt people with. That was forcing her hand.

Or was she a fool to throw away the chance of a new life, for a mere two weeks work with a girl she wanted to help?

Could she leave Australia? Go to a country where she couldn't speak the language nor understand the customs? Could she trust this man...this prince?

Her nerve endings waved in distress.

'Well, what would you say?' he pressed.

She knew what. 'I would say I sold my soul to the devil.'

He tossed his head. 'You are being dramatic,' and his eyes no longer smiled. 'Which is unlike you. But would you say yes?'

She stared back at him. Could feel herself weakening under his gaze. Bowing before his will when she didn't want or mean to. She knew how this could end. 'No.'

'Why not?'

She knew the answer to that one too. 'You're arrogant enough while you have no power over me. I imagine you'd be intolerable as my employer.'

His gaze bored into hers. The food sat long-forgotten between them. 'You don't know that.'

'Oh, I know. I'm not stupid.'

He smiled at her and she almost smiled back. 'No, you're not, but what is it that worries you most?'

Everything...nothing. At least nothing she could pin down. 'I could find myself adrift in a strange country without any job. Without finances. Without access to return home.' She shivered at the thought.

'That would not happen.'

'And if I annoyed you enough.'

He didn't repeat his denial. Just rang a bell and Fatima reappeared and began to clear the table.

Carmen sat waiting, left in limbo. Confused at the sudden halt in the conversation. As he probably intended.

No doubt it was all a part of the eastern customs of taking one's time with negotiations. She was more of the thrash-it-out-and-finish-it kinda gal but there wasn't much she could do.

Time passed as options kaleidoscoped in her head in confusing patterns. She was no nearer to a decision when Fatima had finished pouring small gold cups of thick coffee which she placed beside them.

At Zafar's command she left a jewelled coffee pot in the centre alongside a tray of tiny baklava.

'Please, coffee?'

She shook her head. 'Please, finish the conversation.'

He took a sip and held his cup. 'If I promised that wouldn't happen? If I paid what I promised into your bank account here, now, and you would keep that even if the job didn't work out? Plus you would hold the return ticket to use at any time.'

Carmen bit her lip. Ridiculous offer. Surely he was joking. 'Nobody would pay that.' Stop tempting me.

'You say I am a nobody?' The cup went down and his chin went up. Insulted him again. Every inch the prince.

'You are too easy to offend,' she said and then watched him blink, again regather his patience before he finally went on.

'Supplying money is not hard. Finding people to trust is much more difficult.'

She could see his point. But that was the crunch. She didn't trust him. Or perhaps herself. Or both of them. 'You may have decided to trust me but it's not mutual.'

He brushed that side. 'That is not necessary. I have given my word.'

She didn't laugh. Could see he meant it. Just wondered if his interpretation differed from hers.

What was she thinking even considering this? She wouldn't fit in. Then again what did she have to fit in with? 'And what of your henchman? Yusuf hates me.'

That perplexed him. 'This worries you because…?'

She guessed it was unlikely Yusuf would do anything his master wouldn't like. But she didn't need any more pressure. Doing it for money was bad enough. 'Let's not talk about it anymore. I'll think about your offer.'

To her relief he agreed to leave the subject for the moment.

Outside ca lit the street below and the airport across the bay. An aircraft thundered down the runway and took off. Like she could do very shortly if she went with them to Zandorro. Heading off to who knew where. Did she want to follow that aircraft into an unknowable destination? Could she put her destiny into the hands of strangers?

She wasn't sure when that concept had shifted to a possibility. He asked about where she'd travelled to. Mentioned places he'd lived. Charmed her. But in the back of her mind she was considering her choices. Opportunity or risk?

The talking stopped.

The silence gathered around them. It was late.

She had to get out of here while she could.

CHAPTER EIGHTEEN - Zafar

Carmen looked away from him to her watch. Her eyes widened and she rose to her feet. 'I must go.' As if suddenly woken from a dream. A dream she needed to outrun. A dream he had been drawn into with her.

Zafar too, glanced at his watch. Frowned. It was early, not nine. He'd savoured her company, understood her a little more, wondered about the destructive power of her bad marriage.

Yes, he could admit to himself there was danger in knowing too much of this woman and that his interest was not a culmination of abstinence. The moral issues of being attracted to Carmen – someone other than the woman he had vowed to stay faithful to – and where it could lead...that is what worried him.

He needed to think this through. Maintain distance. Especially if she agreed to join them as his employee. He believed she would come. Probably not for him but because she would worry about Fadia. And that was where he would apply the pressure. 'I apologise for keeping you late, but one question before you go.'

She paused and turned on her way to the door, eyebrows raised in query.

He caught up with her before he spoke. 'Do you have a valid passport?'

'Yes, I renewed it last year. But I haven't agreed to go with Fadia.'

'You have less than a day to decide. We leave for Zandorro tomorrow afternoon at four. If you decide to help Fadia there are things we must arrange.'

'Don't count on it.'

'We will see.' She would come. He lifted her hand to his mouth, felt her resistance, fleeting and then gone as if her body wasn't listening to her commands.

Head tilted, watching her face carefully, he turned her wrist and brushed her skin with his lips. She inhaled and he looked to her forearm where gooseflesh appeared like scattered drops up her arm. Almost imperceptivity she trembled. But he knew.

He smiled as he straightened. '*Fi aman illah*. Go in God's keeping.'

'Goodnight,' she said without looking at him. But not moving. As if she couldn't make her feet move. He knew the feeling. Zafar wanted to slip his arm around her shoulders and pull her to him. He wanted to take her wrist again and savour the taste of her skin, the scent of orange on his lips as he pulled her into his body.

Such poor timing to feel alive again.

A time of great danger approached and he had failed to keep those he cared about safe once before. He would not allow this to happen again.

CHAPTER NINETEEN – Carmen

Carmen didn't know who to turn to. She never asked for advice, something her mother had quizzed her on all through her childhood and later in her teens, but this was too big a risk without some insurance. Someone had to know where she was. And she was running out of time.

As soon as she left the presidential suite she texted Tilly on the off chance she was free. Her friend lived within walking distance of the hotel and they agreed to meet in the bar for a nightcap to hash out her dilemma.

Tilly arrived with her fiancée, Marcus Bennett, head of obstetrics and the man who had been there for Fadia's second son's birth. At least he understood the background.

Marcus dived straight in. 'Tilly says you've had a job offer you're not sure about. With Zafar?'

'Yes.' She hadn't expected this. 'Do you know him?'

'As well as someone can know him. We went through uni together, he worked at the Royal when I was there, then specialised in paediatrics. Apart from his royal duties we usually meet for a meal when he's in Australia.'

Tilly's jaw dropped. 'You still catch up with the prince?'

Carmen brushed that aside. 'There's lots of desert kingdoms and he's not directly in line for the throne.'

Marcus smiled. 'I think he sits third or fourth. So, he's our twin lady's uncle?'

'Cousin. Fadia had been thought deceased but now her two sons are the heirs. Next in line for succession and too important to be unmonitored. He's here to persuade Fadia to go back to her country.'

'She's a widow, isn't she?' Marcus looked at Tilly who confirmed with a quick nod.

Carmen's chair faced reception, unlike the others who had their backs to it, and she saw Zafar walk in through the front door closely followed by Yusef. Seems he'd gone out after she'd left. To do what?

She let the conversation flow around her as she tracked their movements, intrigued by their serious expressions. Her tingly spidey senses warned her that something major was going on?

She put her head down but he'd seen her and even from this distance she could tell he was monitoring her companions. Working out who she was with. She glanced at Tilly who remained oblivious.

Marcus's voice drifted back in. 'Wasn't there a friend involved in helping Fadia?'

'Umm.' Carmen forced her concentration back to the conversation. 'The friendship cooled, I think. Either the shock of caring for twins or I did wonder if Zafar may have bought him off.'

Tilly, oblivious to Carmen's discomfort, was relishing the idea. She hunched her shoulders and lowered her voice theatrically. 'Or threatened him.'

'No.' Carmen shook her head. 'If he'd threatened him Fadia would have run away immediately.'

Marcus laughed. 'You girls watch too much TV. Zafar's a bit stiff but he's an honourable man. One who's had his share of tragedy.'

Carmen listened to the absolute belief in Marcus's voice and let her breath out. Until she saw he was coming this way. She'd needed to hear this positive character assessment before the topic of their conversation came within hearing. 'So, you're saying his job offer would be genuine and reliable?'

'I would say so. Yes.' Marcus nodded emphatically.

Carmen wanted it spelt out. 'And if I don't come back you'll ask him where I am? He'd tell the truth?'

Marcus looked a bit taken aback by that question. 'Are you concerned you might disappear or be abducted?' He smiled. 'I think you're being over-dramatic.' He nodded again. 'But yes, I believe you would be safe and Zafar is an honourable man.'

That was it then. She couldn't not take the offer when it would solve all her money problems in a couple of weeks. She'd just hope she didn't inherit another dilemma worse than money. 'Thank you. I really appreciate your advice.'

Tilly rubbed her hands. 'So, when do I get to meet this prince?' Just in time for Zafar to hear. Carmen winced and looked up.

'Perhaps you could introduce me to your friends?' Zafar stood above them, quite splendid in black. Yusuf three steps behind watched Carmen impassively.

Marcus stood and turned, and Zafar smiled with delight. He held out his hand. 'Well met, Marcus.'

'Zafar.' Marcus gestured proudly. 'Allow me to present my fiancée, Matilda. Tilly's a friend of Carmen's.'

Tilly was blinking and Carmen smiled sourly to herself. She knew how that felt. Zafar lifted her hand and kissed Tilly's fingers. Not her wrist, a little voice gloated, and Carmen frowned at herself.

'Congratulations on your engagement. I am amazed my great friend Marcus is engaged to Carmen's friend. This is excellent.'

Yeah, right. Carmen watched Tilly's eyes glaze over and felt slightly better that even a woman deeply in love could be knocked askew by Zafar's charisma.

Marcus filled the awkward silence. 'Carmen says you've offered her a position for a couple of weeks in Zandorro until Fadia's babies are settled.'

Zafar glanced at Carmen. 'I am glad she is considering my offer.'

She met his inquiring look with a bland face. 'I'm setting up a safety net.'

Zafar raised his brows and spoke to Marcus as if the girls weren't there. 'These Australian midwives are feisty are they not?' Baiting her and aware she knew it.

Marcus smiled down at Tilly. 'I'm living dangerously and loving it.'

The conversation moved on between the men and Zafar and Marcus became immersed in the topic of hospitals. Tilly caught Carmen's eye as they both sat down. She winked and Carmen had to smile.

'So?' Tilly whispered. 'You're going?'

'I guess so.' She shrugged. 'I feel better that he knows Marcus and there's a big bonus that will clear my feet and then some.'

'I'm glad. You're killing yourself here and you've always enjoyed travel.'

'Not in the royal entourage.'

Tilly grinned. 'And now's your opportunity to do just that. What an adventure!'

Carmen had to laugh. Maybe it was exciting to think about being whisked somewhere without effort. Without worrying about the expense. In fact there was no maybe about.

Suddenly it was easier to let go of the responsibility to work everything out for herself, something she hadn't done for a long time, and when she glanced across at the men Zafar was watching her.

A reminder that she was fooling herself thinking that this will be effortless. There would be cost.

The next day proved a whirlwind of formalities made more intricate with her joining the party so very last minute. Carmen only had time to glimpse Coogee Beach receding in the distance as they drove away; she was too busy checking her handbag and list to make sure she had everything.

Her leave from work had been smoothed by the fact she hadn't taken leave for so long. She'd been waved away with little censure of the short notice. Carmen couldn't help wonder if Zafar had spoken to the hospital as well.

The hotel had said return when she could. All too easy. Or maybe nobody would miss her?

Even Donna had said, 'Enjoy, you lucky thing'.

Carmen couldn't help feeling she'd been manipulated by a force that was stronger than she realised. Zafar.

They'd left Coogee in two cars, which shouldn't have surprised Carmen and added that tiny hint of needed reality. Being relegated to the secondary car with the twins and Fadia put her firmly in her place.

Der. What did she expect? Riding with Zafar?

Of course, she was the glorified nanny.

Thankfully the babies were remarkably settled and Fadia had accepted the inevitable.

Now the decision had been made, Carmen was glad she'd come to support the young mother and help her as she became reacquainted with her homeland. Despite Zafar's assertion he would not force the widow into anything she didn't want, Carmen knew Fadia worried. Apprehension and new motherhood felt a recipe for disaster.

They both knew he would have other matters to distract him and Fadia's problems could be overlooked.

Carmen watched s Fadia's hands twisted and untwisted in her lap. 'What is your biggest worry about returning to Zandorro?'

Fadia's hands stilled and her fingers spread. 'It's been six years since I left with my mother. I'm nervous about meeting my grandfather again. He is a stern and politically powerful man. But Zandorro is becoming a more progressive country, not as traditional as our neighbours, but there is friction and the threat of violence between the two countries.'

'Violence?'

'Not war I do not think, or I would not have risked my sons. But danger comes in many forms so we must be vigilant.'

Oh my, there'd be so much she wouldn't know about a monarchy ruled desert state. Would never know. Never understand.

Carmen smoothed her own seatbelt. 'Zondarro is going to be removed from what I'm used to.'

The rest of the short trip to the airport passed silently.

Once they arrived, Zafar, or more likely his staff, had arranged for them to slip through diplomatic transfer to their private jet. Inside, seemed surreal to Carmen, with leather seats, stunning carpets on the floor, gold and crystal and polished wood.

'Would you like something to drink before takeoff?' The immaculately dressed hostess hovered as they settled into their own alcove of seating and Carmen looked towards Fadia who shook her head. 'No, thank you, we're fine.'

The woman inclined her head. 'We'll be taking off in ten minutes.'

Not too long to wait, then. Surely, she was doing the right thing. Carmen shivered as last regrets surfaced. It was momentous to allow herself to be whisked off to an unfamiliar country with people who played by their own rules. Perhaps with the possibility of it not working out. But she did have Marcus and Tilly as a safety net.

Fadia seemed disinclined to talk and Carmen hoped the young mother would close her eyes and relax. Fadia needed her rest whenever she could take it. All Carmen could do for the moment was check the babies and later through the flight ensure they were fed, changed and settled again.

Carmen glanced across at the boys in their capsules strapped to the opposite seats. Two little heads tilted towards each other, matching frowns as if they were squinting to see through the hard plastic sides of their beds. Maybe reassure each other during their first trip in an aeroplane.

She smiled at her whimsy and gradually she relaxed. Allowed herself the freedom to be excited by the prospect of a new country. Delighted to be finding out more about these fascinating people. Just so long as she wasn't focussed too much on a particular mesmerising man.

Except he had changed her life.

Zafar had fulfilled his obligations, paid her debts, provided her with a commercial air ticket to return if needed, and now it was for Carmen to fulfil her duty as assistant to Fadia.

And she would, diligently. There was no doubt in Carmen's mind that Fadia would be better away from the suspiciously behaving Hassan. Hopefully, full support of Fadia's choices would be forthcoming from her family.

Hours later, in one of the waking times, the women were drinking tea after the babies had been fed. Fadia had related a humorous incident she remembered from her life in Zandorro and the young mum looked much more relaxed. Carmen had shared a few amusing hospital incidents and they were sitting in companionable silence. Carmen wondered, 'Why did your mother leave?'

Fadia sighed. 'Her marriage made her unhappy. As she had no son she was allowed to choose to leave. When I was fifteen, she divorced my father. Always she said she never wanted to go back and here I am doing just that.' Her chin rose. 'But I must do so for my sons and their heritage. I hope it's the right thing to do.'

'Did you want to return at all, before now?'

'Once or twice. I have fond memories of my childhood. But it is a big thing to lose my new life in Australia. Yet, I see the advantage for my sons in Zandorro.' She sighed heavily. 'I do wonder what is there for me? I am constrained by my station. Will have choices taken from me. Last time I had been betrothed to a man I never saw. Thankfully my mother paid back the bride price from Australia, so he has no hold on me. But there is worry.'

Carmen struggled to understand the concept of arranged marriage, something well outside her experience. Everything Fadia spoke of was new, interesting or very unsettling. But Fadia seemed happy to talk and finding out more would help when they arrived. She encouraged her. 'Where did you meet your husband?'

The young woman smiled sadly. 'At university in Sydney. We were both studying pharmacy. He was three years older but I was young to have started university so we were in the same lectures.' She lifted tragic shoulders. 'We fell in love. Too short our time together. He has gone without even seeing his babies.' Her eyes glistened. 'All I have left of him are my sons.'

A large tear slid down each of her cheeks and Fadia passed her tea to the discreet flight attendant. 'I think I will try to sleep again.'

Fadia turned away in the pod the staff had prepared for her and lowered her back. Carmen handed her cup away too. She slid down under the thin but warm blanket and lay her bed flat.

Zafar would need to create a supportive environment for his cousin. She hoped he had some plan for long-term support because Fadia deserved warmth and love in her life.

They arrived in Dubai for refuelling twelve hours after take-off and the high temperature shimmered off the tarmac. Outside the windows, robed figures seemed to float around their plane, maybe on flying carpets of heat Carmen thought, fancifully.

Zafar had disembarked without glancing at her and she stifled the disappointment, not for his company, honestly, but for not having a chance to at least see the airport. But they were ushered to a small private waiting room off the aircraft while it was refuelled.

She'd never flown this route. She consoled herself she would see the sights – or at least the airport shops – on her way back in a few short weeks.

Both women had slept well in their turned down beds between tending to the babies. With Carmen's help, Fadia and the boys' routine had become swift and efficient, so despite the distance travelled,

Carmen, who would normally have done a night shift anyway, at least felt rested, pampered, and ready for her first sight of the desert.

Mid afternoon Dubai time they prepared to leave for Zandorro and Zafar boarded the plane just before they took off.

Fadia followed her gaze. 'He does not see us now that he has achieved what he came for.'

Carmen glanced at the girl. 'That was the only reason he was in Australia? To find you?'

Still, she watched her cousin. Eyes narrowed. 'And to bring my sons home. He is a man who achieves his goals. Most men from my country have a singular focus. Though, Zafar has a kindness not often seen.' Now she looked at Carmen with warning in her eyes. 'My mother would say, all Zandorron men use any means needed to achieve his goals.'

Carmen glanced away from the concern in Fadia's eyes. Unease prickled. 'Do you really think so?'

She was not afraid of Zafar. More of her own weakness around him. She stared at the window but all she could see was the reflection of her own face. She knew Zafar's will was strong, but so was hers. Carmen had friends in Australia who would make sure she returned, and Fadia knew the territory they were entering. They had each other. There was comfort in that.

They'd left the azure blue of the Mediterranean and soared over mountains craggy with rock. Soon the sands of the desert stretched as far as the eye could see, undulating like a golden ocean, shimmering with stored sunlight that would cool quickly.

'It's stark yet beautiful. Much larger and more remote than I imagined.'

'The desert has great majesty,' Fadia said. 'But it is a furnace by day and freezing at night. I think I prefer the sand of Coogee Beach.'

The words were said as a joke but Fadia shifted uncomfortably after she spoke, pulling at the neck of her gown. Her bodice bulged at the front of her dress with a new mother's engorgement. 'I may explode.'

Carmen smiled, wanted to hug her – carefully. 'No problem about the boys going hungry. It will pass soon. In another twenty-four hours you'll be so much more comfortable again.' For now, Carmen thought, it did look very tight and painful in Fadia's body. 'I'll ask for another cold pack.'

She raised her hand and the hostess appeared within seconds. They'd been sliding cold sports packs, wrapped in napkins, down the front of Fadia's dress for relief against her now hot and aching breasts. Her milk was coming in.

'Is it nearly time to feed them again?'

'Not quite. Both boys have their eyes closed. Probably another half an hour before they wake.' Fadia nodded and closed her eyes as well.

Carmen glanced at the sleeping boys tucked into their travel capsules and stared out the window again. She'd travelled a little with her parents, but those happy days seemed from another century. Everything had changed when she'd married. Too soon, too rushed, after her parents death. She wished she'd chosen more wisely or chosen a man of honour.

Marcus said Zafar had honour. Carmen doubted she would be here if her gut feeling about Zafar hadn't agreed with Tilly's fiancée.

Or had she allowed herself to be swayed the intense attraction she felt for him?

No. It wasn't like that because she wasn't getting involved with Zafar. This was a job. She knew better now. Which was lucky, as since they'd left it was obvious she had slid down the totem pole.

There was no doubt Zafar had changed since they'd left the hotel and not only into flowing white robes. He'd distanced from her, created a barrier through which he didn't see or hear lesser people like her.

She wondered if there'd been more to the Hassan saga than she'd been told. Big surprise there she hadn't been included. She was really having difficulty with this servant attitude she needed to acquire. The thought made her mouth twist. Get used to it.

His persona of the prince who travelled with entourage, immersed in business documents at the front of the plane, was daunting even for her. It seemed obvious his plan was she'd take the whole problem of Fadia and her sons off his hands until the girl settled into Zandorron life.

Then again, who was she to complain of that because he'd paid handsomely for just such a purpose.

She'd been the one who'd sold her soul to clear her debts and start a new life. As long as she didn't throw her body into the bargain, and certainly not her heart, then it was worth the price.

Carmen wished she didn't feel so unsettled by Zafar, the man outside of the trappings of wealth, the one who had lost his family, had walked on the cliffs with her, had kept her safe in a storm. Or almost safe.

Yet, that awareness of him as a man seemed to grow insidiously despite her reluctance. She knew where he was, who he conversed with, and what held his attention in the aircraft the whole time as if a second screen was behind her eyes telling her.

Those tempestuous moments in the park were hard to banish especially when she could see him, now, up the front of the plane. Larger, luxuriously, living his life.

Her gaze strayed to the glimpse of his aristocratic profile as he turned to speak to the stewardess, the distant deep timbre of his voice barely audible. She felt herself warm at the memory of the way he'd bent her back over his arm and kissed her.

Was she mad? What possessed her to have followed him to a land where his power was absolute?

Stop. You've settled this. Everything will be fine.

Carmen reminded herself to breath. In and out slowly, three times, and relax. Calm. She had control of herself and that counted. She was just feeling a little overwhelmed. Tired. Had been reckless in a storm. Once.

That was all.

But everything seemed surreal when travelling with Zafar. Her father had been well travelled but Zafar travelled as a royal and there was a huge difference.

Though she suspected, clothed in rags he would still be commanding, and she couldn't deny she felt drawn to the man regardless of his station. Drawn but resistant. Immune. She hoped.

Calm. She'd be totally professional, cool and collected. And she was not going to think about the way he had kissed her or why.

CHAPTER TWENTY
– Zafar

Zafar put down the papers he'd been battling with and tried not to think about the woman at the rear of the plane. Or about the melding of their bodies in a storm.

Just what would happen if he summoned the midwife to his on-board bedroom? Fireworks – as a given.

Yet it was as if stepping onto the plane meant the time of pretending he was not fiercely attracted to her was past. Which was why he would not go near her for the flight.

While most of his attendants had dozed during the long flight he'd prowled the cabin, had looked down on her once as she slept in her pod, realised it was the first time he was privy to that view and vowed to himself he would have at least one night where he could drink his fill of the sight.

He could picture her now, her thick lashes curled on her cheek, that beautiful mouth soft in repose instead of militant the way he often saw it. The blanket, fallen to her waist had left her vulnerable, but that strangely only made him lift it to cover her. Not like him at all.

He smiled at the mental image and other memories flickered past like film. A first drift of orange blossom from her skin in the lift. Her scent. Sharing peace with him.

That first glance of hers, a base recognition he couldn't deny, augmented when she'd settled beside him on the floor and touched to share her calm.

A cameo moment when she'd hugged the woman in the park – imparting her strength to her like she had to him during his weakness in the elevator – a moment he still didn't understand. Mostly, recognition came with that wild kiss in the storm that had rocked him. He remembered every second of that with absolute clarity.

Interesting, phobia wise, that this morning when he'd unconsciously pressed the button and descended to depart the hotel, it seemed that his elevator aversion had been put to rest. Because of her? Or because he was moving on and creating new moments of life instead of dwelling on death? Even his fear of heights had receded a little.

Not huge events but remarkable and requiring thought.

Still, there remained a lot on his mind.

Fadia's ability to settle in Zandorro with her heir sons, the kidnap attempt Yusuf had discovered with Fadia's 'friend' just a weakling pawn in a larger plan. He'd quashed that risk but information had been gained that put his grandfather, in fact his entire family, at risk as well.

Yet still, a corner of his mind had been building with anticipation for the moment he had Carmen in his country, his palace, the chance to show her the sights and sounds and scents of Zandorro. To see her smile.

Normally he worked right through these flights.

'Can I be of service, Excellency?' Yusuf hovered.

'No. Rest yourself.' Yusuf nodded and subsided but when Zafar glanced once more at Carmen he noticed his manservant's eyes follow his.

Another memory clicked. She was right. She was not a favourite with his man. He would need to watch that. He fixed his gaze on Yusuf's face and spoke softly but clearly. 'I will hold you personally responsible if she is not happy in the palace.'

Inscrutable, Yusuf nodded. His man had allies in the palace but Zafar had many more. Many, many more.

CHAPTER TWENTY-ONE — Carmen

They landed not long before the sun set above the surrounding mountains outside the main city. The waiting limousines, complete with baby capsules, whisked them through several miles of desert hills to the massive gates and into the turreted city tucked behind by a towering stone wall.

Dark faces peered at them from doorways as the vehicles climbed curved alleys and Carmen acknowledged with a sinking heart it would be difficult to find the way out again.

She turned away from the window. That was okay. Really it was. She would be fine. She'd be able to leave any time she wanted. Zafar had promised.

Thankfully she became distracted as they rounded a bend and ahead the palace shone as if positioned to receive the final light in the country through a break in the mountains. She couldn't help her indrawn breath.

Rooftops shimmered in a blanket of precious metal vying for space in the skyline with domes, towers and minarets reflecting the sun. Golden turrets glistened and one soaring tower in the middle with arched windows and a spire that reached for the sky watched over all.

'It's beautiful. Look at that tower.'

Fadia's solemn face made Carmen pause. 'Yes, it is magnificent as always. I just hope I have done the right thing.' They both glanced again at the soaring splendour.

Harrison stirred and Braxton opened his eyes. Even Fadia's tiny sons seemed alert to the moment.

'Your babies sense something's happening.' Carmen leant over and patted their blankets but it was unnecessary, the boys didn't cry. They lay in their capsules awake and alert as their car pulled up behind Prince Zafar's.

A solemn manservant, accompanied by two older men, opened their door.

Two older women stood behind the men and Carmen could only guess they were here to help with the babies. The castle steps loomed away to the huge front door at the top where a long line of servants stood waiting to catch a glimpse of the royal heirs.

'You take Braxton, I'm taking Harrison.' Fadia had decided no stranger would carry her boys and Carmen was glad to see her eyes brighten with intent. 'They can take the bags.'

Carmen obligingly leaned across and extricated Harrison from his capsule and handed him to his mother and then lifted Braxton for herself. 'No problem.'

'We are here. I hope you are all not too fatigued?' Zafar stood outside the car, waiting for them to alight. He held out his hand to her. She'd expected him to stride ahead.

Had he grown taller again or was it just the backdrop of the palace he belonged in. He waited. For her?

'Good.' He didn't look convinced. 'Very comfortable, thank you. Both princes travelled well.'

'I am sorry I did not speak to you.' His nearness lifted the hair on her arms. 'I have many concerns on my mind.'

Maybe she was wrong and she wasn't invisible. She frowned at him. 'It must be good for you to be home.'

He nodded. 'Rest today. We visit the King tomorrow.' He moved away to be greeted by the dignitaries lined above them.

Carmen looked across at Fadia only now alighting from the other side, and the young mum's wary mood seemed improved by the excitement of arrival. Perhaps she'd have a chance to talk to Zafar about that later. For the moment it seemed they had to run the gauntlet of the stares.

To Carmen's relief they were whisked in a huddle past the greeting party and into the palace while Zafar remained behind as minions from everywhere descended on him. Carmen wondered just how unimportant she would feel in the time she stayed here.

Carmen, Fadia and the boys were shown to a wing of the palace, solely theirs, with their own guards outside the door. Carmen's room of course much grander, more sumptuously decorated, than she had anticipated though pleasantly cool. It looked out over a tiled courtyard far below graced by a tinkling fountain.

With a sinking feeling she realised how small her voice would be amongst these people, especially when she couldn't speak the language, if they wished to exclude her.

Her head lifted. Not the right attitude if she wanted to help Fadia keep control of her boys and her life. And that was why she was here. Her quest. Her promise.

But, she thought wryly, as she put her handbag down on a marble stand, she'd never had a room so huge or opulent. The boys' room took up almost a quarter of their floor nestled as it was between the two women.

A maidservant dressed in flowing chiffon pants and over shirt bowed and offered to put away her clothes. Carmen glanced down at the one small case she'd brought and shook her head with a smile. 'I think I'll manage, thank you.'

She knew her few toiletries would be lost in the marble bathroom and her clothes would hang pitifully in the cavernous walk-in closet. She needed to remember they'd all fit perfectly into her one-bedroom flat when she returned home.

Good thought. And true. A needed dose of reality.

When she crossed the grand expanse of the room to hang her two dresses, she found that the closet already held clothes. At least half a dozen silk camisoles in varying lengths, sleeveless, short sleeved and long, hung with matching trousers in soft shades of blue and green and lemon and even a longer black version.

'His Excellency said you may wish for more comfortable clothes in the heat. Until the palace seamstress has your measurements she has sent these.' The girl cast an expert eye over Carmen. 'I'm sure they will look very pretty.'

'I'll probably wear my own clothes.'

The young girl smiled and bowed her head. 'As madam wishes. Excellency said it is to be the young nursemaids who will help, so it is I and my sister who will be your assistants in whatever you wish for the young princes.'

'Thank you. I will tell Princess Fadia.'

When the girl left Carmen peered through the open door to the boys' room where Harrison yawned and searched for his brother. Braxton lay wide awake in his huge cot. Her feet sank into the luxurious carpets that overlaid each other like pools of shimmering colour. It seemed sacrilegious to walk on such beauty.

'Perhaps you babies can spend a bit of time lying next to each other. Your beds are huge.'

Deftly she changed Braxton's nappy and popped him in Harry's bed unwrapped and legs kicking while she did the same for his brother. Then she lay Harrison by his side and watched them turn their heads toward each other. Harry touched Braxton's face and his brother smiled. Harry kicked him. Carmen laughed.

Fadia's room door opened and the new mum came in. She looked tired but a small smile lit her face as she saw her boys together. Carmen drew her to the boys. 'Look. I swear your sons are more handsome every day. And there's only us here and two young girls who will do as you wish. Everything will work out perfectly.'

'It seems so. But I'm glad you're here. When you go I will be one - alone. Pray they won't marry me off like a parcel.' She clutched Carmen's sleeve. 'Being here makes me miss my husband.' Very, very softly, she said, 'And my freedom.'

'You're tired and nervous.' Was Fadia feeling the weight of the palace too? 'That's to be expected. But perhaps for now, this is better than being alone on the other side of the world. Maybe even at risk of people who wish to harm you or your sons. Anything could happen to you there with no protection.'

The girl nodded. 'My boys are safe. That is good.'

Despite the positive words, Fadia still looked lost and sad. Carmen drew her closer and hugged her. 'I'm glad I'm here with you, until you feel settled. You're a wonderful mother. So loving. Your husband must be smiling at your beautiful boys.'

A whisper of sound and then a voice. 'I agree.'

They both jumped at the unexpected words from Zafar, who had appeared as if by magic in the boys' room. He strode across to Fadia and took her hand.

Strangely, his cousin didn't seem disturbed by his unheralded entry but Carmen was not so sanguine. A knock would have been nice even if it was the boy's room and not hers. She held her tongue but would mention it if she had a chance to speak privately with the intruder.

Even she suspected it wouldn't be smart to chastise a prince in front of servants. Kiri, the maid, followed him with a tray of light refreshment.

Zafir was saying, 'I am sorry for your loss, Fadia, and understand it is not easy for you to return without him. But I will try my hardest to help you be happy here.'

Fadia turned tear-filled eyes towards him. Very softly she said, 'We will see how good your word is.'

Then she picked up her skirts and disappeared into her room. The door shut behind her with a definite snap. Carmen winced and wondered how that would sit with protocol. Zafar's eyes narrowed and his posture stiffened.

Subtle disrespect for his authority – in public – and the maid's gasp ensured more than those in the room would hear of it.

Since her arrival she'd become more aware by the hour of Zafar's power in his own palace. From what the maid suggested Zafar's authority seemed almost as great as his grandfather's and at this moment his cheeks looked chiselled from the same stone as the mountains she'd seen on the way in.

Unable to stop herself Carmen dived into the fray. 'Of course she is upset about being here. She's tired, hormonal and been away from Zandorro a long time.'

He raised haughty eyebrows then clapped his hands and Carmen's brows went up as the maid ran from the room. Okay then.

He turned back to her. 'She does not need your championing. She is as royal as I.'

But not as fierce looking.

His brows dropped lower. 'Why look at me like that? As if I would throw her in irons.'

She couldn't help being a little relieved that had been said out loud. 'You should see your own face in the mirror. Pretty scary.'

To her surprise he smiled, although grimly. 'First I am a cowboy and now I have a scary face? You are the strangest woman.'

'No. Just different.' She gestured to indicate the room. 'Like I see more clearly you are different - in your own palace.'

'No doubt of that.' Zafar strode to the window and then turned back to her, clearly exasperated. 'I am a civilised man.'

When he wanted to be. Of course he was. 'I'm sorry.' She tried her own smile. It had been a silly thought. 'Thank you. It's reassuring. But this place can be a little overpowering.' She glanced around and then back at him ruefully. 'And I don't like the feeling of being overpowered or insignificant.'

'You would never be insignificant.' He shook his head and the last of his anger faded as he crossed the room until he stood a few feet in front of her. 'I do not fully understand you, Carmen, but I doubt the strength of an empire could overpower you if you felt strongly enough.'

Did this man really think that about her? It was a hefty compliment that came out of nowhere and she couldn't help the glow it left in her.

Maybe she needed to explain that. 'Once I was overpowered, and I vowed I would not let that happen again.'

He stilled, and then nodded and she felt he really did understand. 'That has made you strong. I respect that.'

'Honestly?'

'By my honour,' he confirmed, pausing before he went on. 'Tomorrow, when we return from my grandfather's audience, and after the boys are fed, Kiri can mind them for an hour or two while I take you both for a tour. It will be good to remind Fadia how beautiful Zandorro can be. Help her to settle in.'

'That sounds sensible.'

He didn't look pleased at her response. 'I had hoped it would fall less on the sensible side and more on the enjoyable.'

Despite his flippant comment he still seemed worried about something and she hoped it was nothing Fadia should know. 'When she has settled you promised not to arrange her into a marriage?'

'You may not think it, but I do feel her pain. The loss of loved ones.' He lifted his head and stared at her as if determined to say the words to her face. 'I buried my son. Prepared his body and lay him on his side with my own hands facing Mecca in the warm earth. I knew then I could never face the fear of that loss again. Could not face the failure of keeping those I love safe. Who am I to ask another to do the same?' His voice dropped even lower. 'I do understand.'

She believed him. But it hurt, when it shouldn't matter to her at all, to see him still so badly wounded by his past. 'I'm sorry for your loss but glad you will protect Fadia.'

'I will do what I can. But she should know I do not have the final say.'

She let her breath out with relief. 'She's no girl now. She's a widow with children. And a princess. Life has been hard on her but she is strong, too. With the strength of a princess. She just needs time.'

He sighed. 'Again, it is not I who has to give her time. Already there has been some talk of an alliance for her. Our grandfather believes the sooner she has a man to care for the better she will be. I have counselled otherwise and for the moment believe I will prevail. The King is not an unreasonable man. We are to discuss it again tomorrow morning before the audience.'

Still, Carmen thought, with Zafar on her side Fadia would have a strong champion. Carmen had faith in him, unsure where such faith had come from, but she didn't doubt his intent to protect his cousin.

She crossed to the boys. 'Fadia does feel safe here.'

'As she should. We discovered this Hassan you spoke to had hoped to hide Fadia away while he bargained with me for her whereabouts. He was part of a cell that seeks to bring down our government. She was in danger.'

She couldn't say she was surprised but it gave her the shivers to hear it out loud. 'I barely met him.'

He raised his brows at her. 'But you would have hidden their plans from me.'

'Not hidden.' But perhaps she would not have tried to prevent Fadia if she had wanted to run away.

'You need to understand. It is different here. Risks are greater. I fear greatly that Fadia's husband's death was no accident. Knocked down by a car nobody found. What if she was expected to die with him?'

Hit and run? Her breath caught. Poor Fadia. She had thought illness not accident had killed the boy's father. She should have asked. And he suspected Hassan had been involved in that? Who were these people that could discuss death and murder so easily? 'Did you force him to stay away?'

'It was suggested, strongly, that he and his cohorts leave my cousin alone. But I believe we have not seen the last of his ilk. They are eager for a chance in the kingdom.'

She was coming to understand more than she wanted to. 'But what if Fadia decides to return to Australia?'

He dragged an exasperated hand through his hair. 'For the moment she must stay here.'

'You can't make her stay if she's unhappy.'

'A woman's view.' He looked away and again she felt there was something he kept from her. 'Now I do not know why I am discussing this with you. You discuss emotion.'

She straightened. Narrowed her eyes and held his. 'Because I'll tell you the truth when everyone else is too scared to disagree.'

'True. You say you are not afraid of me.' The way he said her name lifted the hairs on her neck. His words seemed gentle but his eyes had darkened, his jaw hardened, and he felt larger as he closed the gap between them. 'That is right, Carmen?'

Just a tinge of danger and perhaps she should choose her next words a little more carefully. It was different here. Tilly's Marcus had suggested she tread carefully until she better understood the culture. She should have listened.

Zafar wasn't finished. 'Not afraid from the first moment we met, were you?'

And suddenly it was back. That tension between them, like the glow from a hundred candles slowly lighting a room. Like a storm raging overhead in a picnic shed, a moment in a lift, the brush of his lips on the inside of her wrist.

'But then you have not been in Zandorro long enough to learn our ways.' He stared at her mouth. 'You will.'

Yup. He'd made her uneasy. Not quite scared the pants off her but almost.

CHAPTER TWENTY-TWO -
Zafar

Zafar understood western women more than she realised. During his years at university in Sydney, he'd enjoyed the company of many fellow students. But this woman was different.

He could see her genuine wish to help others and her zest for her work, her integrity, and yet he could see the fire within. A fire she has no idea she held or the passionate woman she could become for the right man. A fire that matched his in a way he had not expected. Or dreamed of. He wanted to see it.

He watched her search for words to lessen this pressure between them and it amused him that she who lived by diffusing tension had momentarily lost her touch. Bravado was all she had left.

'No. I'm not afraid of you.'

She wasn't. He saw that. And he was glad. But he had her off balance. Like she had him also teetering in a strange place.

'You were the one who said the strength of an empire would not overpower me if I felt strongly enough. I do feel strongly about protecting Fadia. That's why I'm here.' Her voice rock solid.

He stepped closer. 'I am powerful.' A slow leisurely perusal of her - head to foot – her posture taut with defiance and he wondered just how cross he could make her and what would happen if he did. 'Are you not here for the money?'

Her eyes flashed. There it was. Fire. The end to holding her tongue. 'Poo to your power.' Her eyes dared him to touch her. 'And apparently money was the only way you could get me here!'

He watched her regret the words as soon as they left her mouth. The professional midwife regretted them anyway.

He had stirred his usually placid Carmen to wrath? This was unfair of him but it proved he did something to her, too. Incited her, well she incited him, and he could barely keep his hands by his side with the need to pull her against him and quiet that delicious mouth of hers with his.

Not a civilised thought she would approve of.

She said deliberately, 'Your friend, Marcus, said you were a man of honour.'

And that was a 'good hit', his friend Marcus would say. He smiled. 'That was in Australia.'

'Honour is honour.' No backing down. So different from any woman he had desired. Ever.

'We are not in your country now. Here honour and law interchange. Here my word is law.'

He closed the last space between them, captured her gaze with his and held it with the easy power of generations of royalty.

'Your law is not my law.'

He saw it. Felt it inside himself. Some foolish pride, some devil inside, that refused them both to step back. 'You are in Zandorro now. It is your law for the moment.' Then softly. 'Come here.'

She blinked. He saw her disbelief. Incredulity. She'd decided he'd lost his mind. He feared he may have.

'I doubt I could get much closer without bumping into you.'

'Try.'

He could feel the crackle between them. Did she feel it? The air shimmered, thick with vibration that wasn't all words and power struggle, more at stake here than pride and stubbornness. Both of them hot and bothered and pushing for who knew what.

She lifted her chin. Her body dared him to step into her. She glared. 'You might be living under an ancient thumb but I am not.'

She stepped back. Met his eyes unflinchingly and then, as if to save them both from doing something foolish, one of his nephews cried.

The noise escalated. An impatient roar. A little like his own behaviour. His sanity returned.

His nephew could lift the roof of the palace with his demands. Zafar's heart contracted and he turned to look at the babies. This was why she was here. So he could protect them with his life. As would the woman even now turning to her charge.

She took the few steps to the ornate cradle and picked up the child and lifted him like a shield. 'If you'll excuse me, Prince Zafar,' her voice very dry, 'I will take Prince Harrison to his mother.'

He watched her, even with a glimmer of a smile, he nodded once. 'We will return to this subject another time.'

'I don't think so.' She said as she walked away but his eyes followed her until he turned.

Zafar strode away. Annoyed with Carmen, annoyed with himself for playing cat and mouse and having a ridiculous argument when what he wanted to do was feel again the rapport they'd had in the park. All he'd succeeded in doing was alienating her. Of course, she was there to stand up for Fadia if she thought her badly done by. What did he expect? He'd paid for that.

But he was doing the best he could. Had used all his persuasive powers with his grandfather. He would just have to try harder for Fadia. And be more patient with Carmen – and with himself.

CHAPTER TWENTY-THREE
– Carmen

Carmen heard the swish of his robes as he left. Her breath whooshed out. She leant heavily against the doorframe, her legs weak, and clutched the baby. Took several clearing breaths before stepping around the corner to take Harrison into his mother.

All through the feed her mind turned and whirled. What had she fallen into? And just how reliable was this man's honour? And how reliable would hers be if he took her in his arms and bent her back.

Fadia chose to retire early. Carmen decided bed was a safe place, a haven, and a good option for herself as well. She didn't sleep well.

The next morning after breakfast she received a message via Yusuf that Prince Zafar wished to see her. The manservant and the midwife eyed each other, and she thought of her little can of dye. Smiled. Yusuf smiled grimly back.

She was taken to the library off the huge, tiled entry and through a massive, studded door. The room had long arched windows that opened onto a terrace and inner courtyard with the largest fountain she'd seen yet. The tinkling of falling drops filled the room with a background symphony as she crossed more carpets that shimmered and glowed like pools of coloured light, each more beautiful than the next.

At the back of the room ceiling-high bookshelves circled the wall.

It could have been an overpowering room with murals and giant urns, except none seemed to have the magnificence of the man standing in front of her in full traditional robes. He suited the room too well.

'How did you sleep?'

How did he think? After the first two hours it took her to banish their last encounter. 'Fine, thank you.'

'And my nephews?' He was to be solicitous this morning?

She answered calmly. 'We have a routine. Necessary with twins that are breastfed. They sleep longer at night.'

Still, he watched her. Did she have a smut on her nose? 'And they are growing well?'

She glanced around the room looking for clues to this conversation. 'They certainly seem to be. I need scales but as long as they're giving us plenty of wet nappies a day they're fine.'

He nodded decisively. 'I will have scales sent to the nursery.'

'As you wish.'

He allowed himself a small smile. 'Now was that so hard to say?'

She stared back expressionless. 'Am I allowed to ask what happened with your communication with the king this morning?'

'The king has agreed to leave Fadia in my hands for the moment. Which is why I have summoned you.'

She let him get away with summoned because this was much more serious. 'Has she been reassured?'

'I will inform her this afternoon before our audience.' He walked to the window and looked out. 'We meet now to arrange tomorrow. Of necessity our trip will be short. I wish to know if you have a preference for the souks or a drive around the city to see a broader example of the sights?'

'Perhaps the sights, and at least then I may understand the city.'

'As you wish. The city then. Taqu, my friend, also a prince, wishes to accompany us.'

'Does Fadia know him?'

He splayed his fingers on the desk. 'No. Though he was originally betrothed to Fadia before her mother left. He is a good man and wishes to see her.'

'So at least she knows him?'

'They have never formally met. He wed but is now a widower like myself.'

She remembered Fadia's words. 'Her mother returned the bride price. Is this a trick to have them meet?'

He shook his head. 'What faith you have in me.'

Yesterday, she did have faith. Before their discussion and they both behaved badly.

'No,' he went on mildly. 'This allows my grandfather's wishes to be upheld and to take pressure off Fadia because Taqu is aware she does not want to marry.'

She could see a long game ahead but at least he was Zafar's friend. 'What's he like, this Taqu? What makes you think she'd even talk to him?'

'He is not old or unsavoury.' He smiled as he turned back to face her. 'Though, as a friend of mine, perhaps he is a little old in my cousin's eyes.'

She had to smile back. 'Not too old then.'

'My thanks. Sadly, Prince Taqu's wife passed away in childbirth, which for someone in our profession leaves us feeling helpless.'

Her breath caught.

It seemed Prince Taqu had his share of grief too. 'I'm sorry to hear that.' She watched his face. 'When you say our profession, is Prince Taqu a doctor too?'

'He is. But I was referring to your midwifery as well. Taqu has taken over the running of my children's hospital. He has a young daughter and knows Fadia is kind.'

Carmen's brain worked it out. 'Should the unlikely happen, and Fadia and this Taqu fall in love and marry, then have children, doesn't this mean you will be further from the throne? Fadia's new husband would as guardian of her sons, until Harry comes of age?'

'That is correct.'

'And you don't mind?'

'Not at all. It places me another step further away. A step closer to return to my work. Zandorro has already lost a future king. Now, when the time comes, if Fadia does not remarry, my brother will act as regent until Harrison is fit to be king in his twentieth year. When Harrison has children then I am further removed.'

'Don't you want to be ruler?'

He shook his head. 'It was never my place. If my country needs me I will be there of course but I long to return to my work.'

She watched his face change. His eyes brightened and she felt a kinship towards him for a passion shared. This was the man from that clifftop walk in Coogee, a man far-removed from this exotic kingdom.

'One day soon I would like to show you. I have great plans for my oncology research. Critically ill children can never have enough chances of cure. If it is my destiny, I will be able to return to the world I love.'

The inner light extinguished. The impassive prince returned as he pinned her with his gaze. 'I asked you here for your thoughts. Will she come willingly? How you think Fadia will take this?'

'Unimpressed.'

He smiled cynically at her, 'Succinct,' and paced some more.

Carmen sighed. 'She's brilliant with the boys but she is worried about how much control she will have over her life outside of being their mother. Sending her to meet this Taqu means she has no say.'

He stopped and she could see he was considering her words. Trying to see what she was seeing. 'I remember Fadia as a quiet but cheerful girl, shy smiles and even shyer laughter. There was a time we had been close.'

Carmen rubbed her forehead. 'This could really upset her.'

'My cousin had suffered the same pain of loss that I have and shouldn't suffer more. But Taqu is a good man. And will help watch over her if I am called away.' His gaze held hers. 'I need you also to be vigilant.'

'I'm with her always.'

'Yes. And between us we will see if we can return the smile to Fadia's face. But for today, my grandfather wishes to see his heirs. I will send ceremonial robes for them to be dressed before lunch. The audience is at one o'clock.'

She'd bet that wouldn't be fun. For the babies or their mother. 'Of course. I will see they are dressed.'

'I would like you to come.'

Carmen wondered why. 'If you wish,' she said, referring to his previous comment.

'As you appear to be compliant this morning, is there any chance you would wear the clothes in your room?'

She glanced down at her tailored slacks. 'Not appropriate for a Royal Audience?'

'I'm sure my grandfather would understand if necessary. That remains your choice. If you do not wish to accept clothing from me you could always wear them while you are here and leave them behind when your tenure is complete. We would donate them to the needy.'

'If I may leave the clothes here, I'm happy to fit in with everyone else.'

He didn't look at her as he concluded, 'You may even find our style of apparel is better suited to our climate than yours. Everything has a reason in Zandorro.'

Dryly. 'I'll try to remember that.'

He didn't comment on that. 'Tonight, you are both invited to dine with the women. All are anxious to meet you.'

The women. The harem? Or the female relatives? Either way, she was the hired help. 'And you?'

'I?'

She raised her brows. 'Who will you be dining with?'

He smiled. 'I will be dining with the men. But after the meal tonight, I will bid goodnight to my nephews, and shall call for you. There are things we need to discuss.'

'Another summons?' More high-handed demands? 'Perhaps it could wait until tomorrow?'

'Tomorrow we will see the sights we discuss tonight.'

The King sat on a gilded throne at the end of a long hall. From the breadth of his shoulders Carmen gathered he must have once been a large and muscled man like Zafar but his hands and wrists were twisted and thin with the passage of years beneath his flowing black robe.

To her surprise his face, though deeply lined, looked wise and not harsh. She hadn't expected that.

Two guards – surely Yusuf's twin brothers – stood either side of him wearing the curved swords she'd always thought Yusuf lacked.

Zafar headed their party, Fadia stood proud and tall beside him. Zafar carried Harrison and Fadia carried Braxton. Though today they would be given their Zandorron names. To be used in this kingdom.

'Show me the heirs!' The king gestured for them to approach and much of what followed Carmen didn't understand.

Zafar took Braxton from Fadia so that he held both. He stood tall and imposing, a tiny baby in flowing gold robes cradled in the crook of each arm. The twins blinked and gazed about as if searching for each other.

Fadia watched her sons. Carmen watched Zafar. She saw the fleeting shadow of pain as he held the boys up. He would feel his own loss, his own investment in the future vanished with his family, and she almost took a step forward to comfort him before she remembered where she was. Who she was, and where she belonged, in the scale of this ceremony.

That would not have gone over well.

Carmen closed her eyes. So much pain in this family. It seemed she didn't hold the franchise on angst.

After a few minutes of discussion with Zafar and Fadia in their native language the King waved his hand at the boys.

'Hmph.' The old man sighed. 'I congratulate you on your fine sons, granddaughter. They look healthy but must be renamed. In respect of your wishes, and in honour of their father I name the future king, Hariz, meaning strong, a ruler's name, and for the second born, Ba

Leegh, meaning eloquent and level of thinking to support his brother.'

He waved his hand at Zafar. 'They may go.'

Zafar signalled Carmen to approach and between them Fadia and she carried the boys from the throne room.

Huh. Audience over, great-grandsons checked and accepted, and she and Fadia could just toddle off while the big boys talked. How her life had changed since she met these people. But never boring.

So, how much input had their mother had in her sons' renaming? Perhaps Fadia did wield some power. An effort had been made to compromise. Hariz for Harrison and Ba Leegh for Braxton. She wondered whose idea that had been and secretly – and foolishly – hoped it had been Zafar's.

She followed the royals back to their quarters. With every hour she realised how insignificant she was in the palace and this made her more determined not to be overwhelmed. Her sympathy lay even more strongly with Fadia.

In a moment of trivial idiosy she wondered what Zafar's name meant. Probably big of chest or something.

She chuckled to herself and Yusef turned and glanced at her. She smiled at him and he stared stonily back.

'Please follow.'

They tailed Yusef obediently back to their wing of the palace. She couldn't help wonder what she'd do if Zafar went away. Apart from Fadia, she had no other allies in the palace.

After Fadia and she had attended to the heirs, removing their ceremonial robes and replacing them with day wear, Carmen walked to the palace garden to gather hanging fruit for her and Fadia's afternoon tea. Carmen had decided that the sticky almond cakes provided didn't sit as easily as a freshly picked orange did for her.

Soon it would be time to prepare for dinner with the women and then be ready for her audience with Zafar. She would do as asked, on the small things, it was the large issues she wanted to win.

Like making sure Fadia was happy, and that she, Carmen, made it safely home when all this was over. With her debts paid and her heart intact.

All excellent goals she would strive for.

The meal with the palace relatives turned out to be a noisy, opulent smorgasbord of side dishes, fruit drinks and curiosity from mostly kind and interested women on a floor full of cushions. Nothing like Carmen had ever been invited to.

They questioned her in perfect English about her life, her marriage, her divorce and her work. But they had thrown Fadia into disarray about tomorrow when at the end the women had congratulated her about the king's plans for her to meet with Prince Taqu tomorrow.

When it was over and they'd returned to their rooms, Fadia paced nervously twisting her hands as they waited for Zafar.

She'd been upset but trying to hide it. Obviously feeling trapped and tricked by everyone knowing she'd be seeing the man she had once been betrothed to. Carmen had very tactfully mentioned again the benefits mentioned by Zafir as they walked, but had backed away when Fadia had spat her disgust.

When Zafar came to bid his nephews goodnight, Carmen watched as he did what she hadn't been able to, soothing her in a voice calm and gentle against her pain. 'You need a friend as well and he is a good man to keep others at bay. You can deal well together without pressure. I give you my promise I will protect you from coercion.'

One of the boys whimpered and she left the room to check them. When she came back Fadia looked more composed as Zafar held her hands.

Fadia nodded before she pulled away and looked with distress at them both. 'I'm sorry. I'm so emotional lately. My poor babies will think their mother is always crying.'

'It is early days,' Zafar said gently. 'You have been through much in this last week. Be gentle with yourself.'

She nodded, turned her tear-stained face away and walked quickly from the room. Carmen moved to follow.

'Wait.' Zafar put his hand on her arm and motioned for Kiri to follow his cousin. 'Will you walk with me?'

'Now?' It was late. Fadia was upset.

'Why do you always say 'now?' when I ask you that?'

'Because you ask at the strangest times.' And possibly I don't trust myself not to follow you into a deserted bedroom somewhere, she thought. She sighed. 'I'm worried about Fadia.'

He shifted until he could look into her face. 'As am I. But Yusuf will remain here and apprise you if you are needed. Kiri will help with my nephews while you are gone. Do you not need a moment to think of yourself?'

'I'm fine.'

'Fine. Always fine.' He shook his head. Lifted his hand as if to move again that strand of hair but didn't complete the action.

'It will all be as it should. Trust me. One day she will be happy again. Later tonight, I will remind Taqu of the limits for tomorrow's excursion. He is my friend and a good man and knows we are keeping the king appeased. I will ask him to be very careful.'

'Shouldn't you be telling Fadia this?'

He looked down at her. 'I have. But I need you both comfortable with him.'

He shook his head as if at an unpleasant thought. 'I must go away for a few days soon and you would both be alone until I return. Taqu will be an ally while I'm gone. I believe you can better settle Fadia's disquiet. Please ask her not to worry and try not to think about reading anything into his presence. I will talk to her again.'

Carmen nodded and Zafar went on quietly. 'Will you come with me now.'

She said, 'Am I safe?'

His eyes softened. Darkened. Her belly kicked in response. Yup. Danger.

But he said, 'Now is not the time. Should such a time come, when you agree, then there would be no safety for either of us.'

Well, that was warning her.

She looked at Fadia's closed door. 'Their mother is still unsettled. I need to be here.'

'As I said, Yusuf will find us if we are needed. I wish to show you something I think may help you and I won't have a chance tomorrow. After that I will be busy until I leave.'

And when he left Yusef would go with him. 'Very well.' She glanced down at her clothes, worn for dining with the women, filmy swathes of fabric that made her aware of her own curves and left her with little armour to shield herself against this man. 'I'll get a scarf.'

He held out his hand. 'Your clothes are perfect. It is too warm for more.' Strong fingers closed over hers and it seemed her brain shut down as well. She went. Her heart thudded. Not wise but willing.

He took her through the palace, through a dozen different turns she would never remember until they came to a courtyard, the tinkling of the fountain the only sound as they stepped out into the moonlit night.

'Where are we?'

'At the south wall. The vehicles enter by the north gates and climb the hill.' He strode to an external wall and an archway with a door and selected a large brass key from a ring of many such keys. 'This is the other side of the palace and there is no descent to the desert from here.'

He gestured for her to precede him and they came out onto a walled ledge that hung over the cliff. The shimmering moon-bathed desert lay before them hundreds of feet below.

In front and below her lay miles of undulating dunes, expanses of sand and rocky outcrops, all ghostly silver in the night so that she felt they were the only living beings as far as the eye could see. As if they themselves were on the moon.

She slowly turned her head and sighed. 'It's incredible.'

'When I can't get away this is where I come. The place I find some peace if only for a short time.' He lifted his hand and pointed so she followed the direction in the silvery light. 'Can you see that small hill under the moon to your right?'

It was surprisingly easy to distinguish. 'Yes.'

His voice lowered. 'There my family lie. I tell you not for your sympathy but because I am more at peace than I have been since the day I lost them. It began that day in the park, with new life unexpected yet beautiful, and you have helped me towards healing with your kindness to others.'

'Thank you for sharing this with me.'

'I know our ways are different, and I know you try hard to understand. But I want you to know that I see you. If it seems I am ignoring you, or have forgotten you, that is not true. I owe you much. While I am gone, you may like to come here and find peace for yourself. Kiri will show you the way.'

It was as if, finally, he allowed her to see a tiny part of his mind. And his heart. And she wondered how hard it had been for him and how much the darkness out here had helped.

She took his hand and laced her fingers through his and when he bent his head she lifted her lips and kissed his cheek. She wanted to do more than that but it was time to go before she did something she regretted.

'Please take me back to Fadia.'

For a moment she thought he would protest but he didn't. Just nodded. And teased. 'As you wish.'

CHAPTER TWENTY-FOUR -
Carmen

When Carmen woke to the sound of Hariz in the morning it wasn't his usual royal demand. It was a primal screech that made her throw the covers and slip from the bed in a dead run.

'What's wrong, little man?' She picked him up and glanced across at Ba Leegh just as Fadia arrived. Hariz's twin brother lay pale and still in the bed and Carmen's heart thudded with horror as she thrust Hariz into his mother's arms and scooped little Ba Leegh from his bed and tipped him over her arm to tap his back.

'Lights,' she called and Fadia hurriedly switched them on. 'Get help. Tell them to get Zafar!'

Fadia ran into Kiri coming through the door, and sent her to find help. Her other son she clutched to her chest as Carmen lay Ba Leegh down on top of the padded dresser and tilted his chin up a little to open his airway.

No chest movement but his pale skin felt warm as she searched swiftly for a pulse in his neck. Faint and slow, less than sixty, so obviously not her heart-rate she felt, but such a relief to have something to work with.

She puffed two quick breaths over his mouth and nose, watched his chest rise twice, then began to compress his little sternum with her first two fingers. One, two, three, four, until she reached thirty and then two more breaths. All the while the pounding of her own heart threatened to drown out the world as the fear rose.

Zafar swung through the door, Yusuf and Kiri on his heels and he moved in smoothly beside her and took over the cardiac massage.

Fadia sobbed into Hariz's hair when Ba Leegh's little body twitched and he coughed and began to cry weakly. Carmen bit back her own tears as she stepped away, her hand covering her mouth as the restrained fear rose in her throat like bile.

She opened her arms for the distraught mother and hugged the shuddering Fadia as they stood, clutching hands as they watched Zafar. Kiri rocked. Yusef handed Zafar a stethoscope and Carmen bit her shaking lip as she waited. Zafar bent and examined the little chest front and back and both sides.

Carmen chewed her lip as Ba Leegh's cries grew louder and she hugged Fadia's hand, her own need for comfort almost as great.

Then she saw Zafar's face. Saw his cheeks pulled tight and his mouth work before sound came out. 'Good air entry now. Probably a choking episode. Occluded airway.' He paused he inhaled. She knew that feeling. Much harder to be calm now that it was over. 'We'll take him for an x-ray though.' His eyes sought Carmen's. 'Tell me what you found?'

She ordered her thoughts in her head. Strangely more focussed now she knew Zafar needed her control. 'Pale, blue face, not breathing. Skin warm and heart rate around sixty.'

'Too close.' Their glances met, Zafar shuddered, it was subtle, but she saw it. She didn't think anyone else did but this had rocked him to his core.

Both of them knew how close it had been to the horror of SIDS. Sudden Infant Death Syndrome. His palms came together and he bowed his head onto them. 'Thank you.' His voice shook. He took another deep breath. 'So fortunate you were here.'

'Hariz saved him,' she said quietly. 'He warned us.'

Perhaps it was her imagination but he seemed to straighten but his face remained white and strained, dark eyes still wide with shock. She wanted to touch his arm, pull him close, so she could banish the fear from the past in him, but for now they needed to reassure his cousin.

'Hariz's cry was frantic. He knew Ba Leegh was in danger. His cry woke me.'

'I, too.' Fadia took Hariz back from Kiri, wiped her eyes and hugged her eldest son and kissed him before she handed him to Carmen who hugged him into her chest with her own need for comfort. 'Hariz saved him. I've never heard him cry like that.'

The two women looked at each other and Zafar placed Ba Leegh gently in Fadia's arms then gripped his cousin's shoulder to lend her strength. 'Now he is fine. It seems your sons are designed to give us all grey hair.'

'Thank you, Zafar.' She turned to Carmen. 'And you, my dear Carmen.' She squeezed Carmen's hand in gratitude.

Carmen just nodded and stepped back further and bumped into Kiri who shivered like a leaf in a breeze. The little maid slipped her hand into hers and Carmen, juggling Hariz, hugged her to stop the shudders. She felt frozen on a treadmill of mental pictures. Imagining if they'd been too late. Imagining the unthinkable. Imagining the loss.

She squeezed Kiri's hand once more and turned away, to hide the tears.

CHAPTER TWENTY-FIVE –
Zafar

Carmen's beautiful eyes shone with unshed tears. His own heart ached with imagined loss. They were so fortunate she had been here, had been so quick thinking, and he closed his lids for a moment at the horror that could have been.

He followed her and turned her gently, saw the trembling of her mouth. He took Hariz and handed him to Kiri, the child had been handed from person to person as if all needed to assure themselves he was fine too. Zafar drew Carmen in until she was against his chest. 'Let me hold you.'

Zafar searched her face, could see that shock had set in and he needed to feel her against him and show her how much her quick thinking had saved them all. How bravely she tried to control the shudders that rolled though her body in the aftermath of horror.

His brave Carmen.

'Thank you,' he whispered against her hair. 'Again. For caring for my cousin and my nephews.' He closed his eyes as the scent of her stirred memories of another time, of other comfort, and the strange way this woman felt so right in his arms. 'And for me.'

He spoke into her hair. 'We will take Ba Leegh to the hospital and check his lungs more thoroughly. Would you like to come with Fadia?'

She nodded, her hair sliding beneath his mouth and he couldn't help the kiss he brushed against her hair. Of course she would.

'Then go. Dress. We wait for you and Fadia. We can bring Hariz.' He smiled. 'No doubt he too has concerns for his brother.'

The next hour proved reassuring as Ba Leegh was x-rayed and examined again, this time by the head of the neonatal intensive care, and Carmen was surprised when Zafar suggested they leave Fadia and the doctor to talk while they carried Hariz.

'Distressing episodes like this need discussion, and she needs to ask everything she can. I think she will listen more if it is not I who tells her that all will be well.

Thus, Carmen walked around the children's oncology ward with Zafar, and tried not to think of those few moments in Zafar's arms - to feel him around her when death had been so close - made her realise how precious life was. How easily lost. She shuddered as Hariz slept on his uncle's shoulder and they watched the smiling children have their breakfast.

Inquisitive little faces peered at them from beds and highchairs. 'It's a lovely ward.'

'We tried to make it more like a pre-school than a hospital. Here the mothers can sleep comfortably in their children's rooms.'

'And you designed this?'

'With the help of Dr Ting in Sydney. We had many discussions but it is a first for Zandorro and our staff are very dedicated.'

'And you gave this up when Fadia's father died?'

'It was my duty.'

She could tell he missed it. More even than she'd imagined. 'Perhaps one day you will be able to return.'

'Perhaps.' He slanted a glance at her. 'I'm hoping soon, now. Another time, we could discuss the baby hotel concept and if it would work for sick children. If the whole family could come, and the sick child could visit the hospital instead of being admitted.'

'Of course. I'll look forward to that. For children on treatment protocols I think it could work well. I'm sure it would be less daunting for them without the separation of siblings.'

'Good.' He smiled down at her and she could see how passionate he was about this. 'We will discuss this again.' He looked up as a nurse approached and spoke to him. 'They are ready for us to return.'

It seemed Ba Leegh's all clear had been reinforced and he had an idea Carmen had been trying to distract him from the stress of the morning. Neither of them would ever forget the image of that moment.

The ride back to the palace was quiet but there was a feeling of unity and support for each other that had previously been missing. Fadia kept her eyes glued on her sons and every now and then tears would well and then her glance would sweep between he and Carmen and she would sigh and relax back in her seat.

He and Carmen spoke quietly about the idea of building a child-friendly hotel next to the hospital and time passed until he had them safely back in their rooms in the palace. But always at the back of his mind, Zafar could not lose the memory of Carmen's support in his moment of need, her quick thinking in Ba Leegh's crisis, and her insightful awareness of his pain.

As quickly as possible he finished the multitude of tasks he could not put off before he could return to check on them.

The female servants hovered around Fadia and her boys, and Carmen vibrated a restlessness that was probably due to the stress of the morning and made his brows draw together as his glance lingered on her face.

'Do you feel you could walk with me?'

His heart ached at the need in her eyes but she shook her head. 'I shouldn't leave Fadia.'

'Go.' Fadia waved her away. 'We are fine here and perhaps a walk will help you settle. You have stood and sat a dozen times these last few minutes.' She smiled shakily. 'No doubt your nerves are as bad as mine. The girls are here. We shall be fine.'

Zafar nodded. 'Come. I will leave Yusuf and he will phone me if we are needed. We will return soon.'

She walked at his side through the palace, her hip close to his, her warmth soaking into the cold part of him that was there when he was alone. The ornate furnishings along the corridors were nothing compared to her. Finally his entrance with the ancient carved wooden door flanked by statues appeared and he stopped.

Her eyes widened. Brows lifted. Curious.

Always curious. He smiled. 'My rooms. We will have peace and privacy here.'

She nodded and he drew her through the doors and closed them behind his back. Watched her step away, glance around and then back at him. Her brows lifted. It felt as if he had closed the world away. In a burst of honesty he murmured, 'I need to hold you.'

Without hesitation, she moved into his embrace as if she'd wanted to comfort him as much as she needed the same for herself, and he pulled her in against his chest. The warmth of her made him close his eyes with the wash of comfort and relief.

'Thank you,' he whispered against her hair. 'Again. For saving Fadia, for saving me from another tragedy.' He closed his eyes as the fit of her body against his memories that lingered of their time in the storm.

Her hands tightened and he pulled her in tighter as she murmured, 'It was such a shock.'

He shifted until he could see into her face. 'Yes. Yet you managed. I too need time to soak in the fact that all are safe. You need to let yourself be comforted for once, as well.'

Her lovely face tilted. Eyes searching his. 'You do, too.'

She had seen that. He was beginning to think nobody saw through his façade except her. And she cared enough to want to offer him comfort.

He let the terror swamp him for just a moment – to let it out – a release he needed. 'But for you,' his breath caught, shuddered at the horror of losing BBa Leegh, 'we would be at the beginning of more pain.'

'I was there so I did what I was trained for.' She shook her head, arched back slightly. 'Anyone would have done the same.'

He shook his head. Stroked her face. 'We were blessed the day Fadia met you.'

'Fate.'

'Perhaps. My brave Carmen. I just wish I knew what fate had planned for both of us.' Because the dangers outside the palace were growing as fast as his need to keep this woman safe grew.

His hand rose and cupped her cheek. Less carefully but still leashed, he took her mouth and showed how much he had been rocked by the morning's events. How much in this moment he needed her. Worried for her. In return he saw her own horror and she sobbed once, kissed him hard and withdrew.

She pulled back reluctantly and broke the connection. Her eyes searching his, seeing his pain. And perhaps his fear that she didn't understand.

'Let it go, Zafar. I don't want to think of disaster in this moment.' With gentle fingers she touched his cheek. 'You were there, too. Very quickly to my aid. We save him together.'

'As we are here. Together. And I want more.' He tightened his grip. 'I offer you comfort.'

He saw the moment she decided. The glow and the fire in her. 'And will you take mine?' His Carmen tore his heart with her courage. This was a woman not afraid of choosing.

His mouth came down and she sighed into him, he felt her release, savoured the defeat of her fears, as she absorbed his pain and healed it. Would that he could do that for her and her past. But her hand had slipped inside his shirt and his control slipped and melted away to nothing.

Her filmy blouse fell beneath his fingers, as did his in one quick lift. She tasted his skin, dug her fingers into his muscles as if she wished to soak his strength into hers and gave freely and openly of her own power. He lifted her and she wrapped her legs around him as she held his face against hers.

Such generosity and sweetness he had not expected or even dreamed of.

The world shifted as they turned as one, skin against skin, nothing between them as his adoring eyes skimmed her body. Then a shift, and he could do nothing but glory in his imminent possession as she opened herself to him, her back against the wall. Her soul open to him in her eyes.

The rhythm of their need pounded in his heart until both were lost in the maelstrom.

Until slowly the scattered pieces of them fell to earth like the blown grains of sand. They panted against the wall, eyes wide and shocked at the storm they had created between them, until Zafar carried her across and lay down on his bed with her still cradled in his arms.

When Zafar lifted his head his world had changed. He'd reached acceptance of the inevitable. He needed her. Loved her. She was his to protect. He hoped forever if she would have him.

Yet he was endangered by her in his very soul for how would he let her go? Staring into the shadows of his room with Carmen's cheek resting on his chest Zafar inhaled the scent of her. Stroked the thick silken strands of her hair and a part of him died inside to think of her gone. But until the danger was past she must. For she was his weakness.

What had he done?

A pysical connection that had morphed into a million brightly jagged shards with his foolish pride and idea of perhaps loving her once and banishing her hold from his heart.

The most glorious foolishness of it all was the lack of regret for his heart's decision. He'd had no idea this was how it was meant to be. Or what price he would pay. All he knew was that if he did not return tomorrow he could not regret this knowledge they had shared. As long as she was safe.

Sleep claimed them.

His dreams for once were silent and peaceful.

When they woke she shifted against him. Stared into his eyes with such wonder and joy. Even as her words separated them. 'I am glad. I expect nothing. But I must go.'

His hand touched her cheek and she turned her head. Kissed his fingers. With such tenderness she held his heart.

'Go to Fadia.' Yet even as he said it his hand tightened to keep her in his arms. 'And later I will come to you.'

He captured her wrist and drew it to his mouth. Kissed. 'This will complicate everything.'

Her gaze looked down into his. Wise and whimsical. All woman. Strong. 'Perhaps.' As if she knew this too. 'No regrets.'

CHAPTER TWENTY-SIX -
Carmen

S he saw his remorse. Carmen understood because her mind had already accepted that this man was no ordinary man.

Zafar the prince made her feel like a queen, more woman than one year of marriage, more girl than a decade of flirtation, and no matter what, she would always remember this time of mutual need as part of her destiny even if their future could not lie together.

Later that night he did come to her, but he didn't stay.

He pressed a key into her hand. 'I leave early tomorrow. If I am detained unavoidably—' he glanced away at the windows and then back at her, and she couldn't deny the flicker of unease his words and odd body language caused '—then I would like you to remember there is magic in Zandorro as well as the things you don't understand.'

'I don't understand you, Zafar. What are you saying?'

He sighed. 'If I do not return when expected, I have arranged for you to fly to your own country as soon as possible. In the between time, you may use the east courtyard I showed you as your private sanctuary.'

If he didn't return? Her heart pounded.

'To have you here is a gift I treasure, but difficult times lie ahead. Now, I wish you back in the safety of your own country. As it stands there is no future for what we have.'

Because he might not come back? 'Are you in danger?'

'I have safeguards arranged but I will be safer for both of us if I do not have to worry about you.'

She looked up into his face as he dropped her hands. She could read nothing. His face had changed, hardened, and a prince inclined his head and walked away.

The next morning the sun shone in through the windows when Kiri opened her blinds. 'Good morning, Miss Carmen.'

No. It wasn't. Zafar had gone. Probably into danger.

Carmen felt cold. Which was ridiculous. She was in the middle of a desert city. Eggs could fry on car bonnets.

But in her chest, it seemed her heart lay packed in ice for its own protection.

She had no power, would not be allowed to offer help to Zafar. She couldn't live like that. To be here was to be helpless.

She needed to believe that for her own safety. The safety of her heart. She was just a pawn like Fadia and the twins and even Zafar himself to his kingdom. As soon as Fadia was settled she would go home. The sooner she went home to the world she understood, the better.

Zafar was away and Carmen told herself she was glad. The distance of time allowed her to see how powerless she was. How ridiculous her attraction to Zafar stood in the royal scheme of things. How little future they had no matter how she, or he, felt.

Thankfully, every day, Fadia seemed to recover a little more of her self-confidence and enjoyment of the simple pleasures in her life. She grew more comfortable that Ba Leegh would be fine and not frighten her again. Four days had passed since that day.

Contrary to Fadia's fear, the older ladies in the palace were kind and helpful and doted on her babies and herself. But the biggest change was her acceptance that there had been people who could so coldly plot the death of her husband, and perhaps her babies, and she had done the right thing to come to Zandorro. Carmen began to see the fighting spirit of Zafar's family. And the trials they suffered under.

When the babies feeding had settled to a routine, Fadia grew confident and her sons began to develop personalities that made them all laugh. Their first smiles, the way their eyes followed their mother. Who was impatient and who placid.

Hariz truly was the leader, along with his demanding roar, his little clenched fists waved irascibly when he wished to be fed. Ba Leegh would lie quietly, watching the world, observing, secure in the knowledge his needs would be met in good time.

Carmen grew fonder of the young maid Kiri and her sister and the way they cared for Fadia and her boys. And as the days passed Carmen began to fret at being stuck in the palace.

Almost superfluous in the boys' care, she took to spending an hour each day at the hidden eyrie Zafar had shown her as she prepared herself to return to her old life.

On the fourth day after Zafar left, word came to their wing that Prince Taqu, who had arrived in the palace the day Zafar left, wished to take Fadia and Carmen for an outing to the souks.

'I do not want to go,' Fadia said as she wrung her hands and Carmen tried to calm her.

'Of course, you don't have to go. We can say that.' Carmen peered out the window, but she couldn't see the forecourt. 'Is that what you want?'

'Yes.'

'Aren't you a little curious?'

'No.'

'Fine.' She walked to the door. 'I'll go down to apologise and say you're too tired today.'

Fadia twisted her hands. 'Do you want to go, Carmen?'

'I'd like to get out, yes. But I can see the souks when Zafar comes back.'

'You could go.'

Carmen laughed. 'I'm sure the Prince would love that. A strange foreign woman instead of you.'

'Let me think. Perhaps he could come back tomorrow and if Zafar is not back—' she shrugged nervously '—we could go out for a short time. I do not like leaving the babies.'

'Of course. But I won't promise anything in case you change your mind.'

Carmen's first sight of Prince Taqu reminded her how much she missed Zafar. The man was tall, not as broad across the chest as Zafar, but a truly impressive specimen and with a smile that promised kindness not greed. She wished Fadia could see that she didn't need to be afraid of this man.

He came towards her. 'You must be Miss Carmen. Zafar has told me about you.'

'Prince Taqu. I bring apologies from Princess Fadia.'

He didn't look surprised. 'And they are?'

'That today she is tired and her sons need her.'

'I am here for a few more days. Perhaps tomorrow?'

Carmen couldn't help her smile. It was too early to be sure that Fadia would, but she liked this man. 'Perhaps. But the Princess thanks you for your kind offer.'

'Does she?' Too polite to disagree with her, he shrugged. 'Or perhaps you do out of kindness. It does not matter. I will return this time tomorrow and ask again.'

He glanced at his watch. 'Please tell Princess Fadia I await her pleasure. Assure her we will go out for a short time only and perhaps a change of scenery will assist in her recovery. And for your entertainment too, of course.'

'Of course. Thank you.'

On the fifth day, despite Fadia's misgivings, she and Carmen visited the souks accompanied by Prince Taqu. Vendors bowed respectfully as they showed their wares, much less vociferous than Carmen expected, and no doubt their escort helped with that.

Although the first day proved very formal by the time the two-hour visit was over Fadia appeared less strained and had agreed to another foray.

The next day, the sixth since Zafar left, saw them examine all the mosques in the city along with a leisurely lunch at a city restaurant.

Prince Taqu had studied at the same university in Sydney as Zafar and his stories of their escapades had Fadia giggling in a way Carmen had never seen.

The one blot on a beautiful day was when Carmen had left the two to wander a little away from them in the souk. She'd been examining a gloriously emerald silk scarf when the hairs on her neck prickled.

She turned her head, searching the strange faces and for a moment she'd thought she'd seen a familiar unhappy face. Hassan?

But then he was gone and she could see nothing unusual. Her unease continued so she returned to the pair at an antiquities stall where they were haggling with the owner. Fadia looked up with smile at her return and then her face paled and she gasped.

Taqu took her hand. Looked behind her.

'Hassan. Behind that column,' Fadia whispered.

Taqu flicked his fingers at two guards that Carmen now realised had been with them at all times away from the palace.

The robed men slipped away through the crowds and she silently called herself a fool for not realising the danger earlier. Zafar had told her to be watchful.

Taqu's asked for details and she had to say she thought she'd caught a glimpse of the man and that was why she'd returned. He nodded, his kind eyes watchful and serious and with speed they gathered their belongings and returned to the palace.

On the seventh day after Zafar left they stayed at the palace. Prince Taqu was to leave the next day, and had brought his daughter to meet Fadi and the boys. They spent much time in the nursery and gardens.

It proved to be a delightful day and by the end of it, Carmen's presence seemed barely necessary. Unobtrusively she slipped away to spend more time at Zafar's balcony over the desert.

She was glad to see Fadia more relaxed and there was no doubt that Taqu had planned a concentrated assault on the princess's defences. His promise to return the following week seemed to be greeted with pleasure by Fadia and already there was a rapport between his daughter and Fadia.

Carmen knew her need to be here had almost ended which was a good thing. Carmen wished that she didn't feel so alone.

On the eighth day, she heard that Zafar had returned and even the sight of Yusuf coming towards her made her smile in anticipation.

'Prince Zafar wishes to see you.'

Her eyes searched the expressionless face of the guard. 'Where is he?'

'The library.'

Soon. She would see him soon. And if they were alone...

CHAPTER TWENTY-SEVEN
– Zafar

Zafar waited. Pacing back and force over the carpets. Unseeing as he strode from side to side. Every morning and every night of the last seven he'd looked to this day.

The day he would return to Carmen but now the day filled him with dread.

Taqu's servants had captured Hassan, who had revealed plans to kidnap Fadia and her sons. And, Carmen. His Carmen was to be taken as well. And she'd been shopping alone at the time she first saw him.

If Taqu hadn't had the man interrogated then Zafar would have been at his throat now.

Imagine if he had not asked his friend to watch over the women while he had searched for the rebel stronghold. He needed to have

Carmen safely back in her own country before the final coup. If he'd realised how dangerous the situation would become so quickly, he would never have brought her here.

The door opened and she was there.

Her face shining, her eyes alight, looking at him as he'd dreamed she would look at him. How had all this happened without his planning? To give his heart to a midwife from the other side of the earth when his own world balanced on the edge of danger.

To fall for a woman who did not understand the dangers. Who had unwittingly exposed his throat and hers with her innocence of the ways of his country. Carmen, his weakness, who could prove his next failure to keep those he loved safe. A failure he could not bear to repeat.

She was so joyful. So unprepared. So precious.

CHAPTER TWENTY-EIGHT -
Carmen

When Carmen entered the library she didn't know what to expect. Zafar greeting her with no smile on his lips or in his eyes, or no move towards her - was not it – so she halted inside the door. The distance between them came as an unpleasant shock.

Yusuf disappeared and she swung back at the noise of the door closing. Turned back to Zafar. 'Is everything all right?'

'It is time for you to leave.' A flat, unemotional order.

The words like spears from an unexpected ambush and they punctured her euphoria in a heartbeat. Trampled right over her girlish dream of him opening his arms to her and hugging her close. Or more.

Anticipation fell, fluttered in tatters around her slippered feet and her eyes narrowed as she took in his stiff shoulders and tight arms.

Hands behind his back. Something had happened. He wasn't going to share what that might be.

'I am told that Fadia has settled. Her sons are well. It is time for you to return to Sydney.'

She heard the words, glanced around at the opulence of his library, not his rooms where she'd hoped he'd meet her, and unconsciously rubbed her arms. It must have been bad. 'Today?'

'Yes.'

Go home. She'd thought it would be soon but... Leave them all - right away. 'What's the hurry?'

'Danger.' Zafar's dark brows drew together as he looked past her shoulder. 'Your job is done. Your time here is over. And I will have you safe.'

Carmen looked away herself. To hide the shine of tears that stung. Such a fool. Imprudent girl. She'd slept with him and that was that. But in her heart she didn't believe he meant the words. He was protecting her. And his way to do that was to force her to leave.

Of course she'd been waiting like a damsel in the tower for her prince to return. More fool her. Huge fool her. 'As you say, you want me gone, then there is no reason for me to stay.' Still, she didn't want to believe him, so she wouldn't look at him. Couldn't.

She heard him move and her heart leapt. She turned her head but he was pacing, not towards her. Pacing away.

Fool again. What did she think? That she could stay? That the royal family would greet her with open arms because she'd kissed him a few times? Slept with him once.

She lifted her chin. Well, damn him. She was not the little woman. Not the weaker sex. And she felt remarkably, frozenly calm. Maybe she'd been dreaming, and this proved he wasn't to be trusted. She had reason to dislike him now, which was so much safer than that other emotion.

'I have no choice. I will pack my things.' She turned and opened her own door, without goodbye, rudely pushing past Yusef and returning to Fadia's rooms without asking the way, her feet slapping noiselessly on the marble floors making her even madder (where else could you storm off without making a sound) only in a blinkin' place like this, not even giving her that satisfaction. She passed no one.

It all happened so fast after that. Her clothes were already packed when she arrived back at the children's wing. Fadia stood stunned and white-faced, Kiri sniffed and hid red eyes as she gathered the last of Carmen's possessions and purchases.

In the background, having caught up, Yusuf stood with arms crossed, waiting impatiently for her to say her goodbyes.

She was bundled down to the car, and when Yusuf opened the door, he stopped. Stepped back. Seemed very surprised to see Zafar seated within.

'I will accompany Carmen to the airport.'

She hesitated and then slipped inside and settled herself. Yusuf stared at his master for a moment and then inclined his head before shutting the door and moving to the driver's seat.

Her thoughts whirled. Had the situation escalated? Something wasn't right. The car started and within minutes they were leaving the palace behind and she turned back once to see it like a mirage at the end of a cobbled street. 'What is going on here?'

Zafar stared straight ahead. The privacy screen raised between them and the stiffness of the man driving escalated the tension. 'I need you out of the country.' A quick glance at her and in that moment he did not look distant. More torn and her heartache eased a fraction. 'For both our sakes.'

Did she place him in danger? She couldn't help a glimmer of foolish hope that he might not want her to go as he sat beside her in the limousine, with darkened windows shielding them from the world outside. Private and intimate. Silent.

He didn't speak again and she turned to look out the window as they drove through the winding streets. Regretted she'd never explored the city on her own properly. She would have if she'd known she was to be banished at a moment's notice.

As if he'd heard her thoughts. 'I understand you wandered the souks a little with Prince Taqu and Fadia?'

How could he start a normal conversation after the last craziness of leaving? She blew out a breath determined to be the mature one here. 'Yes.'

'If I'd asked you, would you have liked to walk the markets with me? Allowed me to show you the city?'

Carmen frowned. What was that supposed to mean? She glanced at his face for a clue to this sudden change of tack. 'Of course I enjoy your company. I slept with you. What do you think?'

He blinked. She looked away again and a woman dressed in black, with all but her eyes covered, disappeared into a doorway as they drove through the big gates out into the desert.

'I don't understand any of this. This rush. The distance between us. You coming with me to banish me. But perhaps that's just because it's very different for a woman like me to understand your culture and customs.'

'Perhaps it is impossible?' A world of sadness in those words.

'If I'd had the chance, I'd have found it difficult but not impossible.' She shifted in her seat to watch him with more comfort. 'I should thank you. I had the chance to set out on an adventure to an exotic land in the company of interesting, warm and kind people.'

Except he had asked for more. Once started she couldn't stop. 'Remembering of course this was a job that would end.' She glanced away from him to the sand that stretched into the distance and her mouth hardened. 'End suddenly. I am only the hired help.'

'Have you finished?'

She inclined her head mockingly. 'Of course, Your Excellency.'

He ran his hand through his hair, impatient with her, or was it with their circumstances, and she smiled grimly. At least he wasn't immune to how he was treating her.

His voice dropped. 'You are at risk, and I need to have you safe. I will not be responsible for harm befalling you.'

Her chin went up. 'I can look after myself.'

'Not here, no. You can't.' His eyes burned into hers. 'You will leave now and be safe.'

She narrowed her gaze, sifting through the mixed messages, reading between the lines. 'You said I could never be bowed.'

'Listen to me, Carmen. At this moment—'

A sentence he didn't finish as gunshots rang out. Disjointed cracks like stones hitting the side of the car. She'd never heard a bullet strike for real before, but she'd watched enough movies to understand that these weren't rocks.

Yusuf swerved the car onto a side road and suddenly they were airborne as they crashed through the scrub beside the road and into the desert along a barely discernable track.

The screen between Yusuf and them wound down as Zafar pushed her onto the floor and he flattened low in the seat and slid his phone from his pocket. His eyes held hers as he spoke rapidly into it and for some crazy reason she was too angry to be frightened.

'Three vehicles. They will catch us.' He nodded to Yusuf. 'Support is coming. They will meet us at the valley pass.'

'What now?' Carmen asked.

He turned back to her. 'I have arranged for us to be picked up in an armoured vehicle but it is fifteen minutes away. We must quickly hide ourselves. It is too late to get you away. Then we will return to the palace until it is safe.'

She nodded. Time to do what she was told. Maybe prove she could be relied on to do so when in danger.

'If anything happens, and we get separated, keep quiet and unobtrusive and I will find you.'

'This is the rebels who oppose you?'

'The last attempt at a coup. It is almost beaten but I feared this last assault. The last of the tribe have nothing to lose. They wish to capture me but do not worry. Safeguards are in place.'

Now she was more scared. For him. 'I'm not letting you out of my sight.'

'Listen to me.' He grasped her arm and eased her up beside him. 'This is my world and when this is done it will be done.' He dropped a swift hard kiss on her lips. 'Do as I command and you will be safe.'

For the moment the other vehicles were out of sight as they passed a large outcrop of rock and before she realised what was happening the car slowed. Zafar reached in front of her and pushed open the door on her side. She could see the sand rushing by.

'Go,' he said urgently and pushed her so that she slid across the seat and out of the door onto the sand in an ungainly heap. He followed her and Yusuf in the car accelerated away from them in a spray of sand and dust and suddenly the car was gone. She was in the middle of the desert, at midday, and Zafar was pulling her towards a crevice in the rock face.

CHAPTER TWENTY-NINE –
Zafar

Zafar cursed his own stupidity as he shielded Carmen as they crawled rapidly towards shelter. He'd uncovered the plot but thought they had another twenty-four hours before it escalated enough to pose a threat. And he'd dragged his woman into danger because he'd wanted to have her safe on a plane.

He froze. *His woman.* Carmen.

It would be best when she flew home until all this was settled. His Carmen – there again, that proprietal slip – was a resourceful woman but the worry gnawed at him like a rat in the palace dungeons. She might be foolish if she thought he was in danger. All she had to do was lay low and wait to be picked up.

But there was worry that she wouldn't.

The hurt he'd seen in her eyes would pursue him. She didn't trust him now, after all they had gained between them, and he couldn't blame her. He had missed her like a limb for the last absent days until the communication they had captured outlined the revolt. And the plan of kidnapping Carmen to force Zafar's hand had forced him back to the palace.

But the plan of shifting her to safety had backfired so now there was no time for thinking. Only surviving.

CHAPTER THIRTY – Carmen

Carmen heard the growl of approaching vehicles and her heart thumped in her chest in time to the revs of the engines.

'Go,' Zafar's voice urgent behind her.

Spurred into action she crawled forward inelegantly to the outcrop and into the rock crevice, which afforded some protection from the road. She slid deeper than she'd thought she would, several feet down into a heaped pile of sand. It was dim, and something scuttled away from her hand as she tried to steady herself. Carmen shuddered and pulled her hands in close to her chest.

Zafar fell in beside her taking the last of the space.

The roar of the approaching vehicles seemed to vibrate through her body and she blocked out whatever animals or reptiles she'd disturbed as she jammed her head down into his chest and squeezed her eyes shut as if she could squeeze the last crazy minutes away.

They would get through this. That thought at least brought her some sanity. And Zafar's arms around her helped.

'Fear is your worst enemy.' His voice held a hint of humour.

His breath in her ear. She'd heard those words before. Then remembered. The woman on the headland, a test of unexpected birth to go through, and she'd said those exact words to Jenny. He'd remembered.

Well, fear was in this dark and dismal hole right alongside them both and she wasn't happy. 'Who are they?'

'Friends of Fadia's Hassan.'

The cars roared past and the sound bombarded her more than the sand that flew into their crevice and coated their hair and cheeks. Her heart pounded in her ears, staccato thumps, and then she realised it was not her heart but the sound of a battle not too far away. An explosion. Then the whoosh of heavy fire and the rattle of machine guns. Then the distinctive sound of vehicles driving off.

Now beneath her own dread was her fear of what had happened. And even a little trepidation for the annoying Yusuf. Who are these alleged friends of Hassan's? Was he really connected to this attack? And just how out of her depth was she?

Zafar stood after peeling her from his chest. Well the quarters were tight. He reached above and pulled himself up. 'Stay here. You are safe while you remain in shelter.'

And then he was gone.

Leaving her with the previous tenants scuttling against her hand. She shuddered. Zafar's footsteps disappeared into silence.

He'd told her to wait here but the fighting over the rise had been quiet for a few minutes now and she had a bad feeling about the silence. Zafar had said they wanted to capture him.

The tenant, most likely a desert scorpian, brushed past her hand again and that decided her. She was out of here. She pushed up until she was standing and could peer over the ledge. If need be she could come back to hide or get out of the sun but she had to know that Zafar wasn't in danger.

It was easier falling into the crevice than climbing out but with a skinned knee and three broken nails she finally crouched on the outside of the opening. She shuddered as she glanced back into the dark interior. It would take a fair incentive to get her back in there.

The hot breeze dried the perspiration on her face and she licked her lips. Sand grated against her tongue and she could smell the smoke that was rising from ahead.

Thirst was an issue already but not one she could worry about just yet. Keeping low she scurried to the next outcrop and stayed crouched as she listened.

No sound from over the hill and no vehicles that she could hear.

When she made it to the top of the sandy ridge she could see the remains of a recent battle. She gasped when she saw Zafar's car hinged on its side next to another burnt out wreck of a jeep. A collision with consequences and then she saw Zafar edging towards the car. Yusuf!

She scanned for other movement as she skidded down the hill from outcrop to outcrop until she was ten yards from where Zafar crouched. He turned and looked at her, briefly his eyes flared then he sighed and shrugged. 'Of course, you came.'

A low groan made her jump and she flattened herself against the rock and twisted her head from wreckage to wreckage. It came again, guttural, weak, definitely masculine.

Side by side they crawled across the open ground to Zafar's car and peered in the smashed rear window. Yusuf. The man seemed trapped.

Crumpled against the steering wheel and the smell of fuel reeking the air. The burning jeep smouldered too close for comfort.

Together they slid around the underbelly of the car until Zafar could stretch up and peer in the driver's window. 'Yusuf?'

With a struggle the man opened his eyes. 'It is the will of Allah. Leave me.' He closed his eyes and whispered, 'It is too dangerous.'

Typical. She was getting so sick of men giving orders. 'Not until we get you out, she muttered.

She caught a brief grin from Zafar before he said to Yusef, 'Let us see if Allah wants you out, first.'

On its side, the car had one door blocked by the ground and the other in the air. Zafar pushed the car to rock and hopefully make it tilt but nothing happened.

He turned to Carmen and searched beyond her. 'I cannot budge it alone. If we put weight on this side maybe the whole car will fall back on its wheels.'

Away from the flaming wreck beside it. Neither mentioned that. It wouldn't be easy to do that without getting closer to the flames but she didn't need to say it.

As they circled the car the tyres a tendril of balck smoke curled from the nearest tyre to the flaming wreck and time was running out. The building heat encouraged the fire to cross the distance between cars.

'We need a wedge. Quickly. Something to give leverage. We're running out of time.'

'Yusuf.' Zafar's command snapped the man awake. 'Reach the lever for the boot.'

'Leave Excellency. Take the woman.'

'Not without you. Do it. That is my order.'

She heard keys rattle and then the boot latch clicked. Zafar scooped out a large coil of rope and a tyre lever.

'We can do this.' He glanced around. 'That tree. Can you tie it there?'

She nodded, ran and anchored the car to the sturdiest trunk with as much tension as she could manage. She'd always been lousy with knots but the granny would have to do. The rear tyre grumbled into flames and acrid smoke burned in her throat until she coughed.

Zafar took his end of the rope and tied it quickly around the nearest axel to Yusuf.

Flames crackled. Smoke billowed. They weren't going to make it.

She could hear her pulse in her ears as the sweat ran down her face. They were too slow and Yusuf would burn. She'd grown accustomed to having his miserable face around.

'Fear is your worst enemy,' she muttered and gritted her teeth as Zafar caught the rope and twisted it with the tyre lever to tighten it slowly. The rope creaked, the car swung a few centimetres but didn't fall as she watched him strain against it to shorten the rope. She ran back and heaved as well, pulling on the bumper. Between them it rocked and finally shifted.

In the end it didn't need much, just enough to change the centre of gravity, so that when it happened she wasn't prepared and the car swayed and then fell with a whoomph while she landed on her backside with a plop.

Yusuf cried out as he was bounced around inside until Zafar wrenched open the door. An almost unconscious Yusuf half fell onto the road and she ran to help Zafar as the rear of the car filled with smoke. Flames began to lick along the interior roof lining as they dragged him free.

It was going to explode. They'd be caught in it. They needed to run.

She kept pulling, yanking, cursing this heavy lump of a man who had uselessly fainted on them when she needed him awake, but finally he was partially sheltered behind the rocks and trees.

That was when she heard the approaching vehicle. The outcrop that almost protected them was too small to hide behind. Zafar pulled her behind him to protect her with his body.

Would this day never end?

The low throbbing rumble distracted them just as the limousine exploded into a fireball and she ducked her head into Zafar's back. A blast of heat singed the hands she held over her head and then it settled to a steady roar of heat.

The rumble became a throb from the armoured car which had slowed and then stopped beside their outcrop. Please let it be Zafar's back-up.

Two young men with machine guns jumped out of the armoured truck. One ran to the front of the vehicle and the other to the back as they guarded the road. A third climbed down and approached them with obvious relief. 'Excellency. Are you well?'

Zafar turned a blackened face to Carmen and no doubt she looked just as much a disaster. He grinned and she realised the crazy man was on a high. Men!

'It seems so.' He raised his singed eyebrows. 'Carmen?'

She nodded and after one searching look at her he stood up. Then he pulled her into his arms and kissed her. Thoroughly. Exuberantly. Well.

'Go with Allah.'

Was that this man's name or a benediction?

At her obvious confusion he smiled and touched her cheek. 'I must go.'

Strange thing to say. She wasn't planning on staying either. 'Me, too.'

A few minutes earlier for the cavalry would have been nice she thought sourly as she peered through the smoke to the car. Followed the direction of a man pointing to where the unconscious Yusuf had been lifted into a vehicle. She was back in the second car apparently. She felt bedraggled, singed, and over it all.

A vehicle drove off. 'Miss O'Shannessy?'

'Yes.'

'His Excellency said we were to transport you to the airport.'

Now? Like this? Of course he did. 'Yes, of course, but what of your prince?'

'He has already left.' He helped her into another vehicle. I'm afraid your luggage has been destroyed. But we have matters in hand and you must catch the flight.'

He gestured to the front soldier who'd run crouching towards the rise and after a brief surveillance had returned. 'His Excellency wishes you safe journey.'

So - after the drama of the morning – she'd been banished after all.

Carmen flew back to Australia first class from Dubai. After she'd been given fresh clothes and offered a mile high shower. The strangeness of being greeted by name and deference was both unexpected and uncomfortable and a strange letdown after the desert battle.

Yet all that was over-shadowed by the desolation she felt as the distance widened between her and the man she should be angry with. The opulence did nothing to drown out the ache in her heart.

On arrival in Sydney she was greeted by another robed man holding a board with her name and whisked to her flat. But Coogee was filled with memories, and everywhere she turned made her want to run. Hide. And miss Zafar.

She almost wished she could restart her double-shift working life so she could fall exhausted into bed and sleep instead of gazing out the window and thinking of Zandorro.

After two weeks without a word from him, she knew she needed to get away. Maybe one day, when the hurt was less raw, she would return to Coogee but not for a while.

Instead, she tidied up the loose ends of her life, paid the last of her husband's debts, attended exit interviews, finalised the lease on her flat, then written to a friend and was off to explore the outback – now that money wasn't a problem - near Kununurra along the Gibb River Road, and she could stay with another remote midwife. Carmen had attended a course with Sophie Sullivan in Perth once and they'd hit it off well.

She had to go somewhere remote, unfamiliar, safe from memories for the next few months.

Later, when time had passed then she'd see where she ended up. For the moment she needed to escape. She'd arranged for the few sentimental possessions she had left to be stored in a box at Tilly's.

Donna, the concierge, had arranged a farewell morning tea at the Baby Hotel with a few friends from both work places. It was the last thing Carmen wanted but she smiled and nodded her way through the morning, until her head ached as she waited for the time she could pick up her bags and head for the airport.

When she finally escaped up the lift towards the maternity room where she'd left her things, so many memories bombarded her.

Funny how the corridors seemed strangely empty without a man standing guard outside a room.

Before she stepped out of the room for the last time, she dragged open the heavy sliding door to let the stiff breeze from the ocean beat against her.

The wind was up and she staggered a little as it whipped the curtain from beside her and flapped it against her head. The sting of salt lifted her face and she asked herself again why on earth she'd chosen the furthest place in Australia from any beach for her new job.

But she knew why.

She hated the weakness she hadn't realised she would be a party to. Her hands gripped the cold metal of the rail as if to soak in as much of the sea as she could before she left.

'I'd prefer you moved back a little. I've had such bad experience with heights.'

Oh. She didn't turn her head but she'd heard him. Felt him in the stillness behind her. Wanted to see.

Memories fluttered around her like butterflies in the sunlight. His eyes on hers, his wicked mouth curved and coming closer, his angled cheeks beneath her hand. She could see it all without looking. He'd come back to haunt her.

She turned to see Zafar at the door of the terrace. He still hated heights. 'Then why are you out here?'

He moved back a little to safety now that he had her attention. 'Because you won't answer your phone.'

'My phone is turned off. What do you want, Zafar?'

'You.' One word. One command. From a prince.

'Still giving orders? Another quick romp?' She had to finish this. 'Go away.'

He crossed his arms. 'Not until I have had the chance to explain.'

Of course he wouldn't go away. 'No.'

'The flight was long.'

Tough. 'I'm sure there are other business affairs of state you need to do here.'

'I apologise for the delay. But it was for the future. Our future.'

Sadly, she didn't believe him. 'We don't have a future.'

'We need to talk. My suite or yours?'

Impossible man. She needed to get this right. 'I only have this room on loan. It's not mine because I don't work here anymore.'

She stared at him, so tall, so handsome, with his smile glinting. 'Mine then. As you wish,' he said.

See that was the problem. She ducked her head again. This was classic Zafar. From out of nowhere, with a few words – but the right words – he had her smiling. Or wanting to smile. This was his power.

It had to be his room. This place was so much smaller and he would be too close no matter where he stood. And the last thing she needed was another midwife to catch her with a man in here.

'I leave for my flight in twenty minutes.'

'I will need less than that.'

Arrogant. It seemed strange to follow him up the stairs and out into the corridor to his old room. To see no Yusef outside in the corridor. Zafar opened the door himself and stood back to allow her to enter.

She slipped past carefully and he didn't try to touch her.

There were no rugs. Different than before. As if this Zafar did not need to bring extra luxury. She positioned herself in the middle of the lounge area, creating as much space as she could from anything that could hem her in. She saw by his face he knew what she was doing.

The silence wasn't comfortable. 'How is Yusef?'

'He is well. Downstairs in the car.' He smiled and the warmth in his eyes almost blinded her. 'He does not dislike you anymore.'

'Should you be here without protection?'

He shrugged. 'Yes, we are all safe. Finally, for a long time I hope, my country will have peace.'

'And what is your personal goal?'

His eyes bored into hers as he took a step closer. 'I believe you know.'

'No idea.' She crossed her arms protectively across her chest. 'But I do have a plane to catch.'

He spread his hands. 'Your flat was empty. Moved from. I thought I was too late.'

'For what?'

'You are so distant. Yet incredibly beautiful as always. I fear more beautiful than I remembered. How could I have forgotten the way you twist my chest until it hurts?'

So badly she wanted to slip into his arms and bury her face in that particular chest. Breathe him in. Tell him that her fears had overcome her, that she'd lost faith that he would come. But she could not tell him this. No. Not until she knew for sure.

He smiled at her. 'I'm sorry I bundled you out of Zandorro.'

'Ha! Not the only place you threw me out of. You bundled me out of a speeding car.' Yes, she remembered that.

His chest shook with silent laughter at her pretended indignation. 'Because I discovered a plan to use you against me. You were not safe.'

'And would their plan have worked?'

He took a step closer. 'To keep you safe? I would do anything. As you would say, like a shot.'

'Don't talk about shooting.' She shuddered. 'Why are you here? It's a long way to come to say you're sorry. And I need to leave and create my future.'

'I have no quarrel with that.'

She blinked. Then he came closer until he was right beside her. Until his warmth seeped across the tiny gap of air between them. If she weren't careful he would defrost her protection.

'I would like you to leave here and come back to my country. From there decide on your future.'

'I'm not going back to Zandorro.'

'You must. I have great plans to show you my desert.' He took her hand, and she tried so hard not to grip his back. 'Most especially the desert. We spoke once before about the desert but still we haven't slept there.'

The desert. 'I tasted the desert. When the sand flew into my mouth after...'

'Yes, I know. I threw you out of the car. Tsk tsk. So unforgiving. Where is that famous sense of humour?'

He was rubbing her neck. Smiling into her eyes and the warmth was melting her heart. She stepped back. 'You're doing it again.'

'What?'

'Playing me.'

'Come play in the desert with me.'

'You come to the desert with me. I'm due in the Kimberleys and parts of it are very dry.'

She'd love to see his desert. Properly. With him. But she wasn't that much of a fool. She needed to get away. Just standing here talking to him was killing her.

She lifted her chin in renewed defiance. 'Better yet, don't.'

'Is it too much to ask that I at least try to leave you with good memories of my country? Of me?'

Even if she had to lie. 'I have no wish to see the desert with you. I just want you to go.'

He stared at her, narrow-eyed, and she remembered how he'd measured her when they first met. In the hotel. As if he was looking into her skin, into her brain. She tried not to fidget as she forced herself to hold his gaze.

Then he nodded. 'I see.' He glanced at the window and the brightness outside. 'Then at least let me drive you to the airport. I will place my jet at your disposal to fly you to your Kimberleys.'

'I have my own ticket. Thank you.'

CHAPTER THIRTY-ONE—
Zafar

Zafar watched her. This was not what she wanted. This woman who walked unaided from an ambush. Who helped him save Yusef. This was not a woman who ran from life.

Had he discovered his amazing Carmen's only fear – that he may not love her enough?

Ungrounded fear. He would give up his life for her. Everything.

He did not know why she had decided she wasn't going to give him time to woo her. He wanted her. Badly. More desperately than he could remember wanting any woman. And he believed she wanted him. He prayed she did.

Incredible to be so obsessed with her, with the dream of Carmen with him always. The life he wanted to share with her, to return to his real work, for the rest of his life. But life would be nothing without his Carmen.

He needed her by his side. Together they could change lives in his country. Together they could achieve great things for other as well as themselves. A team. A shared vision. 'Or you could come back with me.'

'Why? So you can send me away again when you decide it is too dangerous for me?'

He deserved that. 'I would not send you away again. This time I will go where you go.' His fear had almost cost him everything.

She needed less protection that he anticipated. He would always protect her, his lips twitched, and he supposed if needed, she would protect him. His brave Carmen.

He saw her lack of faith for her standing and he remembered the times he had not explained things when he should have.

'I know it is different for you in Zandorro. As it was for me when I lived in Australia. There are good facets of all cultures and the world will be a better place when we learn to meld and bring the best out of both worlds.'

She looked back at him. 'Do you think that will ever happen?'

'Slowly, but surely.' He smiled and he saw the softening. Allowed himself to hope a little. 'When people work together miracles happen.' He wanted the woman who made him laugh, who frustrated him many times, but who made him proud when she took charge and was brave. He wanted a partnership of equals.

The more he talked the more he saw she remembered their times together. He remembered them too.

The smiling nymph in the water. Caring for Fadia. Saving Be Leegh.

The woman after the storm with her head thrown back and her eyes dark and languorous in his arms. Her gift of comfort when he needed it most.

She said, her voice firm, not shying from the truth. 'I did not have a voice in Zandorro. I can never live like that.'

'I know. I understand those difficulties more than you can guess. I'm sorry you felt excluded. We could work together to change that. Can you trust me?'

'No.'

He sighed but wasn't as downhearted as he could be. This was only the beginning of his siege. He could wait. She was worth it.

'If that is your last word then I will drive you to the airport.'

She frowned. That lack of trust again. Suspicion well-grounded but not in the way that she thought.

CHAPTER THIRTY-TWO –
Carmen

Yusef held the car door open for her, and this time he bowed low to her. Face still inscrutable but his body language was different. She touched his shoulder as she passed. 'Good to see you are well, Yusef.'

'Madam.'

She slid in and Zafar slid in behind her. The leather smelled familiar, the tinted windows reminded her of another limousine, and how she'd thought Yusef would die. How Zafar could have. For all her posturing her pride was nothing to that fear.

He took her hand and kissed the inside of her wrist. Her skin remembered. Her heart rate sped. It felt ridiculously right to feel her hand covered by his. She was hopeless. With his other he gestured to the space around them. 'Now we are alone.'

'Really? Must be a remote-controlled car.' She inclined her head at their driver.

'But that is Yusuf. He is with me always.'

'I noticed.'

He shrugged. 'I have decided to accompany you on your flight.'

She struggled to keep the shock from her face. Now more than ever he mustn't know her thoughts. 'When did you decide that?'

'When I said I would accompany you to the airport.'

It had seemed too easy. 'Why am I not surprised? It seems my instincts to run from you are better than I believed.'

He was amused. Wasn't that lovely. Not. 'Then why did you get in the car with me?'

Stoke up that anger. It was a good defence against the urge to put her head on his shoulder. 'What choice did I have?'

Now he was openly smiling. 'True. None. For I could carry you.'

Too handsome. Too charismatic. Too close to her heart. 'So where are we going?'

He lifted his head and though he wasn't smiling she could sense his deep love of the destination. 'I had planned to propose to you in the desert but cannot force you to leave the country with me. So, we go to your oasis. Your desert camp instead of mine. I believe they have luxury cabins in the Kimberleys. There I will woo you, seduce you and love you, until you have agreed to be with me, and mine, forever.'

'As what?' She raised her brows. Fighting back the excitement as she drummed up some form of defence. 'Am I to be your concubine? Your midwife for nieces and nephews?'

She was fighting a losing battle and she wasn't losing it with him but with herself. She loved him, had from the first, and she suspected she always would even if she never saw him again. She tried again. 'I'm off to visit a friend. I've promised.'

He shook his head. 'Not for a few days yet, your Tilly says. And you could postpone. I wish to share the desert with you. At night.'

She raised her brows. 'Is that all you want to show me?'

His strong hand stroked her wrist. 'What can you possibly mean?'

The conversation was like foreplay. Like a teasing breath on her cheek. Like the squeeze of his fingers against hers. And she loved it. 'Are you sure you're not going to try to seduce me again?'

'I am.' He leaned closer. 'Of a surety. But you would still have the option of refusal. And I will persist until you have banished me or agreed to be my bride.'

So belovedly arrogant. 'You have tickets on yourself.'

'Ah. Colloquialisms. We must teach our children.'

She laughed. Gave up. Leant across and kissed him and he drew her into his arms. She was home. 'Let's not go to the desert here. I will see your desert first and another day we can visit Sophie in the Kimberleys.'

He leaned forward and pressed the button to lower the window between them and Yusef. 'Return to the hotel. We have much to arrange.'

She caught the man's smile in the rear vision mirror.

They stayed in Coogee. Were married quietly in the Presidential Suite of the Baby Hotel as soon as possible. Tilly and Marcus acted as witnesses and then they flew back to Zandorro.

They stopped overnight for the first formal part of the Zandorron wedding, a civil ceremony attended by dignitaries and the king, but finally he could carry his bride to the desert. It took an hour to reach the oasis in his helicopter.

Late afternoon saw them come upon a circle of tents on the sand beside a stand of tall palm trees, ridiculously like a movie set with shaded pool and tethered camels. An outsized tent sprawled in the centre of the oasis and Carmen couldn't keep the smile from her face.

'You did tell me.'

He frowned. 'When?'

'In Coogee.'

He smiled as he remembered. 'Before the birth in the park.' He nodded. 'That is when I fell in love with you.'

He stroked her cheek. 'Tonight, I hoped we could share a traditional wedding night Bedouin style. Our official Zandorron wedding will take place in a month when I can introduce you as a married woman. This night is for us.'

A woman approached, vaguely familiar, and bowed to Carmen and more deeply to Zafar. 'I am Kiri's mother. And Yusuf's wife. My allegiance is yours.'

Zafar smiled at Carmen's shock. 'See, others love you as I do.' He took Carmen's hand, turned her wrist and kissed her as if the caress belonged only to them. 'We will meet again an hour before sunset. Sheba will help prepare your bath.'

Bath? She shivered. More delay. Rituals and traditions that she must now learn. Lessons for the future. She nodded, glad that she had spent some time with the Zandorron women and had an idea of what was ahead but inside she held a little trepidation. She wasn't good at being pampered and by the smile in Zafar's eyes he knew it.

She gazed at her husband, a man she had wed twice already, and still he hadn't taken her to bed.

'Patience,' he said.

Patience would kill them both. But she had to smile. She loved him, would always do so, and she knew, without the shadow of a doubt, he would always love her. But after tonight they would live, wonderfully – she hoped prolifically – between their two countries, and his strong face framed that light in his eyes as he watched her go. Dark eyes that promised the wait would be worth it.

In the two hours that followed she discovered she could learn to cope with the hardship of luxury but the slowness of it would take some getting used to.

Kiri's mother, Sheba, took her robe and helped her settle into a claw footed bath strewn with rose petals and scented with oils that seemed to shimmer in the water. When she left there, she was gently massaged with more aromatic oils and her toes and fingernails painted with colourless shimmer. Her ankles and wrists were traced with henna-coloured flowers and her hair dried and dressed in a coil on top of her head.

Then came the veils. Layer after layer, promise after promise, to lie in wait for her husband to remove. Even the one that covered her face and left just her kohled eyes to stare back at herself, this stranger, this eastern princess she never planned to be but could never regret.

Enough. She wanted Zafar. Didn't just want memories.

Memories of the caresses from their one time together blurring he image of herself in the mirror.

She could feel awareness gathering in her belly and finally it was time to go through to Zafar's rooms. The impatience grew until her breath came fast so she tried to slow her steps, but too long she'd been a doer, used to being busy. This had all taken so long when she knew where she wanted to be.

'Ah, you are ready!' The relief was there in Zafar's voice and she smiled at him. Ha. He felt impatience as well.

'Finally.'

'My impatient wife.'

'My frustrating husband.' He laughed out loud.

'Now I will introduce you to our traditional wedding feast.'

She rolled her eyes and he laughed again. 'Come, eat with me on cushions, drink from my cup and I will drink from yours. We will climb to the top of the dune and you will see the stars from the safety of my arms.'

Now that she had Zafar by her side time passed swiftly. The wine they sipped sweet on their tongues. Almonds and honey with secret ingredients she'd never discover, but its nectar left a trail of heat that coiled in her belly. Warmth spread over her skin until time slowed to a second by second beat of some distant drum in the night.

Tiny bells tinkled in the tent, discordant yet mesmerizing, and music played softly in the background. Zafar offered her morsels of flavoursome meat, tiny slivers of candied fruit, and spoonfuls of rice so aromatic she closed her eyes. Each touch of his fingers to her mouth fired the flame that grew.

When she returned the favour, he supped from her fingertips, his eyes burning into hers but his physical restraint more powerfully an aphrodisiac than if he had taken her finger into his hot, hot mouth.

Never had she felt so aware of a man, so eager to feel his arms around her, so needful to be crushed against him, to be as one...

Zafar rose and held out his hand and as he did so she realised she was healed from the past. Her heart was bursting with wonder at this man who had saved her from the lack of trust in others she had never thought would lift. They would achieve whatever goals were set before them. Together.

'Come, my wife. My love. It is time to begin our life as one,' and she followed him to a platform of cushions set with candles.

Outside their tent, a shadow stood in the distance guarding them silently, as they came together with joy and love and the potential of a new dynasty that promised health and happiness and harmony in the kingdom of Zandorro.

9 780645 278712